A KILLER COMES TO SHILOH

Thunder splits the Arkansas night as the Shiloh death bells toll the frightening news—a mysterious killer has brutally cut down three young lives. Quickly the terrified drive for revenge threatens to destroy not only the town but the nearby peaceful Cherokee nation. Although he is a Quaker, Joshua Shank is the only man strong enough to see the killer brought to justice without any more blood being shed. Until suddenly the killer forces the man of peace into a death stalk—the most savage encounter of Shank's entire life.

A KILLER COMES TO SHILOH

Cynthia Haseloff

GUNSMOKE

First published in the United States 1982
By Bantam Books, Inc

This hardback edition 1997
By Chivers Press
By arrangement with
Golden West Literary Agency

ISBN 0 7540 8007 2

British Library Cataloguing in Publication Data available

Printed and bound in Great Britain by
Redwood Books, Trowbridge, Wiltshire

For my Father

Chapter One

The bells that had drawn Joshua Shank into the blackness of the storm were louder now. Hollow and grim came the sound from their iron throats.

In a flash of lightning Joshua saw the church doors with the death notes nailed upon them. Ducking his head against the rain that blew onto the uncovered porch, he climbed the stone steps. Three notes were tacked to the double doors. The torn edges of the papers flapped as fingers of wind slipped beneath and tore them. He held the lantern high, straining to read the words that washed from the wet pages. The window glass beside the door rattled in the wind.

Josh wiped the rain from his eyes. From the Cherokee script, with English below, he read:

Mary Louise Neil is dead forever. At a murderer's hand. She was a Christian ten years old. Now she has passed from the earth to the place of long rest, leaving behind anguish for the living. Now she has no pain.

The second and third notes were the same except for the names and ages of the children—Jo Belle Walker, age nine; Rebecca Ann Beard, age eight. Josh bent his head, pressing his eyes with his tough brown fingers. Tears mixed with the rain on his cheeks.

"Shank, come inside," Tom Bryan said. "Come out of the weather." Joshua followed him into the church. In the dim light he could see the shoulders of men in the front pews and hear the murmur of their words.

"We don't know it's true," Bob Little said thickly.

"Why would somebody put up something like that on a night like this?" a voice asked from the darkness of a pew.

"What better night for such news?"

"Why didn't whoever put up them notes stay around? That's purty peculiar puttin' up the notes, ringin' the bell, then disappearin'. Like a joke or somethin'." Pettigrew Wills still wore his house slippers. His nightshirt was stuffed into his britches. The red galluses and striped shirt looked gay and bright in contrast to the dark world. "I was here in five minutes. Somebody done his work and left out the back before I could get here."

"Shank, do you figure it's a joke?" Tom Bryan asked.

"I don't know, Tom. Maybe we ought to check the campmeeting before we go any further."

"That's right. We ought to check," Sam Waters said. "Sure. Somebody ought to go out to the camp. All those girls' families were at the meeting. Saw 'em yesterday evening."

Nobody moved to leave the church for the storm.

"I'll go home and get dressed," said Wills. "And you and me can go out there, Shank."

"By the time you get dressed, Petti, we can all go out there and get back." Sam Waters wanted action. Wills' ways were too slow and ponderous.

"All right. All right. But we'll have to get our horses or a wagon or something. Damn, we're all on foot, and it's three miles out there," Wills said.

"Shank, take my horse," said Tom Bryan. "She's fast, and you're the best rider among us. You can get out there and find the truth before we get organized. Rest of your men go on over to the house. Clary'll have coffee ready by now. We can wait over there together."

Joshua followed Tom around the house and into the stable out back. The barn smelled musty like wet hay. Tom's sorrel mare whinnied at them. Tom Bryan acted as mayor of Shiloh. Like Joshua's family he had settled Shiloh when it was nothing more than some strung out farms along the Indian line. He'd started the first store.

"If it's true, Josh—" he thought a moment. "If it's true, we'll have to keep our heads. Folks'll take it mean. Whoever did it will go to the Nations to hide, probably. We'll wire Fort Smith for a marshall."

"Let's be sure first," Josh said, swinging into the saddle. "I'll be back as soon as I can, Tom." He kicked the mare, ducked the door jam and cantered into the rain.

Tom stood in the doorway a few minutes. He watched the other town men standing on his back porch holding coffee mugs. Clary'd have breakfast soon. "Killin's too good for a bastard who'd kill them children," he heard one of them say. "It'll be a pleasure stringin' him up." It had already begun—the quick, blind call of blood for blood.

A faint light was growing as Joshua rode into the meeting grounds. The camp was three miles from Shiloh and no one on the grounds had heard the bells through the storm. A few men were out driving tent stakes deeper and digging run-off trenches. Smells of bacon and coffee came from the women's area. Men could only enter there from an hour after sun-up until an hour before sundown. That was Reverend Poe's rule. The local preachers bowed to his wisdom. Camp meetings could confuse the feelings of believers. And sexual love might be mistaken for spiritual. So the men and women had separate, inviolate areas to insure high purpose.

The Shiloh campmeeting drew families from Arkansas and Indian country mostly. But every year there was at least a group or two from Missouri or even Iowa or Illinois. They were usually passing through Arkansas on their way to Texas. A lot of folks had felt a need to move on after Appomattox. The border country held too many memories, mostly bad ones and moving on seemed the best way to start fresh. A lot of men had gotten religion in the War, too. In leaving home, they looked for special guidance. And the Shiloh campmeeting had begun as a kind of anointing for those moving West and for those turning back to God.

Every year since the War's end, fewer were Westing, but the hunger for benediction and renewal never slacked. At the end of each summer, people came in their wagons with their families to camp for a week along Sleepy Creek and listen to the preaching and the singing, to find again something that couldn't be dug out of the farm or hung up on the clothesline, to let themselves go in the emotion the meeting brought. Some came in superstitious fear and appeasement of the vengeful force they called "god." And some came because the others were there and ripe for picking.

Reverend Poe's tent sat behind the preaching arbor in the trees. Josh walked the mare down the wide aisle between the log benches of the congregation.

"Preacher," he called out.

The tent flap flew open and the shirt-sleeved evangelist offered his tent in a sweeping gesture.

"Get down, brother. It ain't fit to be out." Josh dismounted. "I'm prayin' it'll pass on over before the morning service. There's a lot of sinful souls a needin' salvation. You ain't been around here before, brother, air you?"

"I'm a Friend, Preacher."

"Ain't we all, brother, ain't we all. Set an' eat. Sister Woods just brought me a breakfast that'll bust two bellies."

He sat down and jammed a fork into an egg yolk. The orange-yellow contents oozed onto the plate.

"Love fried eggs. Women is a miracle, brother. To fix a breakfast like this in a drivin' storm."

"Preacher, did you hear the bells?"

"What bells?"

"The Shiloh death bells."

"No, can't says I did." He ran his tongue around his teeth. "You needin' a funeral preached in town? My fee's two dollars."

"We're not sure anyone's dead. The deaths are supposed to be out here in the camp. I've come to see."

"What's that you say?" Preacher Poe stuck a fingernail between his front teeth. "Who's dead out here?"

"The death note said Mary Neil, Jo Belle Walker, and Becka Beard."

The preacher stood up, overturning the table and

dumping the good breakfast onto the dirt. Still holding the fork and wearing his napkin he pushed past Josh and out the front of the tent. He paused a minute then headed around the log pews toward the women's tents. Shank followed, watching the hatless preacher throw down the useless fork and bull through brush and believers.

"They's down here together," he pointed toward a tent set away from the others as he slid standing down the hillside rocks.

By the time he reached the tent, Josh was at his side. They bent together to look inside. Nothing. The tent was empty except for little girl things scattered on the faded quilts—a hair ribbon, a broken comb, a rag doll, a pair of button shoes.

The preacher straightened. "Maybe they's gone to breakfast."

"Look," said Josh, dropping to his knees and crawling inside.

He reached back into the corner and grasped a wadded nightdress. The white garment was wet and saturated with a dark substance. He lifted the rear flap over a muddy set of tracks. "They went out through here," he called back over his shoulder.

In the rain outside again, he handed the gown to the preacher. "My God, that's blood," the preacher said, turning the garment in his hands. Blood, pink and fading, ran with the rain through his fingers and onto his boots.

"What's happening?" a short solid woman with a parasol asked the men contemplating the dress. "My God! My God. That's my Mary's dress—"

Preacher Poe threw his arms around the woman and held her to him. The disturbance drew others from the women's camp.

"Sister Leona, fetch the men."

Mrs. Neil struggled in his arms to see into the tent. "She ain't there, sister. Don't torment yourself a tryin' to see. What's your name, son?" he suddenly asked Josh.

"Joshua Shank."

The preacher's eyes glazed over with a biblical ecstacy. "They're over yonder across the Jordan, brother Joshua. Gird up the fighting men and lead them into the land of our enemy. Smite them. Smite them hip and thigh. Blood for blood. Eye for eye. Tooth for tooth. Kill the Amalekites, Joshua."

By this time, men were sliding down the slope to join the crowd gathering in the rain. "Look," shouted a boy pointing across the creek into the brush. Rain had washed the mud from something beneath the blackberry bushes. "It's a foot." The crowd surged toward the creek bank.

"Stop. Stop where you stand!" shouted Shank. "If you all crush about now, you'll ruin any clues the rain hasn't. You men, take your wives to their tents. The preacher'll tell you who's missing."

In the crowd Josh saw faces of men he knew. "Whiting, Trimble, LeFevre, come with me. Boy," he said to a youngster pulling up the tent flap, "my horse is at the preacher's tent. Ride to town. Tell Tom Bryan, 'It's true. Send for a marshall.' Then bring him back here. Don't talk to anybody else. Do you understand?" The boy nodded and ran up the hill.

"Trimble, get some help and try to keep people off this stuff around the tent. Whiting, LeFevre, let's see what's over there."

Joshua and his men waded into Sleepy Creek. Looking over his shoulder, he saw Trimble and another man guarding the tent. The preacher, still holding Mrs. Neil, was making his way up the rocky slope with the crowd behind him.

"Funny ain't it," said LeFevre. "Half hour ago folks couldn't think of anything but stayin' dry. Now they're walkin' around in the rain, and they don't even care."

There was no further talk as the three men walked up the muddy slope to where the foot had been seen. The body in the brush was that of a girl child, small and pale. The throat was cut out.

"Oh God," Whiting grabbed his mouth, walked a few feet away and leaned against a tree.

"Can you tell who it is, Josh?" asked LeFevre shifting the tobacco from his cheek.

"Jo Belle . . ." The words caught in Shank's throat. He cleared it. "It's Jo Belle Walker."

"What's in her mouth?" LeFevre kneeled beside the naked child and pulled away the rag stuffed into her mouth. "Why it's her underdrawers." He looked up at Josh's pale eyes. "Shank, some son of a bitch used this child for a woman."

"Yes," Josh heard the word croak from his throat. He removed his slicker and covered the mud-streaked body. "Let's try to find the others."

"Shank, over here. Quick!" Whiting yelled.

LeFevre and Shank ran to where Whiting had wandered into the thicket. Under an overhang, out of the rain, the two other children lay.

"They're dead too. Laid out dead," Whiting said.

The girls' bodies were side by side under the shelter, their eyes closed, their hands neatly folded over the night-dress spread lengthwise across the two naked bodies. Wadded rags of their clothing lay beside their heads. Both throats were cut. Shank, Whiting and LeFevre stood with the rain running down their backs. Josh's cotton work shirt clung to his broad shoulder muscles. The men stood without words, staring at the handiwork before them, taking in all the details of the scene, trying to make sense of what they saw.

"Weren't killed here. No sign of struggle," said LeFevre as he looked about. "Must have been put here neat like afterwards." He walked away on the rocky slope. "There's a cave around over here, boys."

The inside of the cave showed where the murders had taken place. Pieces of clothing were thrown against the mossy walls. A length of bloody bailing twine and dark sticky stains lay on the kicked up floor.

"Bastard, dirty child-killin' bastard," said Jon Whiting. "What kind of man rapes and kills children?"

"Be quiet. I heard something move back there." LeFevre pointed to the darkness at the back of the cave.

The three looked at each other, then moved as one toward the back of the cave. Through the black emptiness they saw the mouth of a crawlway leading further into the mountain. Settler boys called it the keyhole because it ran directly through the mountain connecting two caves that opened to daylight on either side of the mountain.

"Jon, circle around the outside," Shank said to Whiting. "She opens at the honey tree. Hurry, Jon. Maybe we can trap him."

Jon wasn't listening for further instructions. At the first words he was on his way. He and the others had hunted coons too often in these woods for him not to remember where the cave opened. They had worked as a team many times before.

LeFevre was in the dark passage ahead of Shank. "Wish we had the guns and dogs."

"I'd settle for a lantern," Josh said crawling on hands and knees through the narrow passage. "We'll be able to stand up pretty soon."

"Yaw, I hate this damn keyhole. Shorts my breathin'," LeFevre grunted. Like Josh, he was a tall man, not used to crawling, suffocated by the tight, damp darkness. "Damn, all I can think about is that nest of rattlers we killed in here when we were kids."

"Think about catching who did this night's work. Wait. LeFevre, you got a match?"

"Hell, Josh, ain't no time for a smoke."

"Something stuck my hand."

Shank patted the damp floor around his right hand. He sat back on his heels, touching the ceiling with the back of his bent head. He ran his hands along the walls, groping for whatever had stuck him. His right hand touched something and a dull metallic clink sounded as the object bumped the wall. He grabbed it.

"Get out of here, Will. I got it, and I'm getting desperate to stand up."

Will LeFevre skittered ahead, clearing the passage for Josh. In a few minutes both were on their feet running with hands on walls as the passageway curved toward the light.

"He's headed for the blackjack thicket," yelled Jon Whiting from the opening.

Shank and LeFevre ran harder, breaking into the rain at a full run. Whiting was ahead, jumping rocks and bushes as he ran. Shank and LeFevre fanned out in the way they had often used hunting, knowing by instinct the positions of the others, surrounding the catch like fingers closing over the palm. Whiting, the center of the group, entered the woods first. He held up within a few feet, listening, looking, waiting for his friends. His gaze ran among the shadows and lights, the straight tree trunks and thick underbrush. Nothing moved. The wood was quiet, silent except for the relentless rain. He looked about his feet for the killer's tracks, but the rocky soil running streams of water told him nothing.

"Where did he go?" LeFevre called.

"I don't know."

"Anything your way, Josh?" LeFevre too had stopped and was listening.

"Nothing."

A few steps at a time, quietly, together they moved over the loose hillside rocks. The rain came harder, striking their faces like needles. The sky was darker again, and lightning and thunder played off to the east.

"Ohhhhhh . . . !"

The sound came from LeFevre. The others looked his way hearing the rocks moving and a heavy thump.

"Help!" he yelled.

They ran.

"Hold him, Will. Hold him!" shouted Whiting.

In a minute they had burst through the brush. LeFevre was kicking and cussing on the ground trying to reach up and free his ankle. He was hanging upside down in a "v" between lichen-covered rocks.

"Goddamn new, slick, damn boots. I busted my own goddamn leg."

"Shut up," said Whiting. "You're making so much noise fifteen killers could stomp-dance out of here. Hell, I thought you was hurt."

"Killers, hell! Hurt! Get me down!"

"Why don't you watch where you're walkin'?"

Whiting scrambled up the pebbly path around the

exposed limestone outcropping where LeFevre's foot was caught.

"Hold your knee, Will," Shank said, lifting LeFevre and pushing him up toward his ankle.

"Pull it out, Jon," he said to Whiting, who was kneeling on the rocks trying to get hold of the boot. He jerked the heel out of the crevice, releasing LeFevre's full weight against Shank.

"Oh, no!" Shank yelled as the weight hit him and sent him and LeFevre tumbling in the mud and rocks.

Whiting jumped up from his place above the rock, fell, and slipped after the two sliding down the hill. Shank, still holding LeFevre, grabbed for an exposed root and missed. He hit a sapling abruptly stopping the slide. He grunted with the impact.

"See anything up there, Jon?"

"No. Didn't see nothing," said Whiting, looking at the body slumped against Shank. "LeFevre? God, he's dead, Josh."

Shank looked at LeFevre's pale mud-streaked face. "No, just passed out. Must have passed out when we pulled him loose. Man, he's heavy," Josh said trying to get out from under LeFevre's bulk. "We'll have to carry him in," he said, looking back up the muddy slope, back toward the silent thicket.

"You're bleedin', Josh."

Shank looked at his hand, turning up the palm to see the wound.

"Look around, Jon. Something stuck me in the cave and I brought it out. Must have dropped it in the fall," Josh said, struggling out from under LeFevre, leaving him lying on his side.

"There's a feather up by that root," said Whiting.

They caught branches and roots and crawled back up the slide, tearing the knees in their pants and covering themselves with red mud.

"It's a knife."

Josh picked it up and held the bloody broken blade flat against his hand as he and Jon studied it. The blade had been long and keen, but was broken three inches from the hilt. Brass bands held the wooden handle together. A feathered charm drooped wetly from the end. The initials "O. M." cut crookedly into the wood.

"That's Orpheus McKee's blade, Josh."

Chapter Two

By the time Shank and Whiting carried LeFevre across Sleepy Creek, he was beginning to come around. "Put me down, damn it. I ain't no invalid. Put me down. I can walk." The pair obligingly stood him up. He brushed himself and tested his ankle. "It's busted. I'll have to lean." He put his arms over their shoulders, and they continued toward the camp. "You bastards dropped me so much I hurt all over." He assayed the long slope ahead. "Hell, everything in this country's uphill, even coming back."

Trimble, whom Shank had left to guard the evidence, now squatted beside the tent. Water ran off the brim of his hat. "You boys look stove up."

All were soaked. Their faces were streaked with red clay. Shank's once-clean shirt clung to his skin. He shifted his weight from the skinned and bruised knee that showed through the tear in his britches.

"What happened?" Trimble asked.

"LeFevre fell over his fat feet just as we had the killer trapped," said Whiting.

"Where'd the killer go?"

"He's still up in the big thicket between the creek and Shiloh Road. Probably lay in there till night," Jon answered.

"All the kids is dead?"

"Yes. Jo Belle's over there." Shank nodded toward where a farmer stood guard over the body. Trimble nodded. "The other two bodies are up near the mouth of a cave. Has Tom Bryan gotten here yet?"

"About thirty minutes ago. Said to leave everything for the marshall. But with this rain, there ain't gonna be much left."

The four men looked up at a noise above them.

"Stop these men here," Tom Bryan's voice rang out. "If this crowd gets down there, we'll find nothing.

We'll destroy any clue the rain doesn't. We must wait for the marshall."

The crowd Bryan spoke of hovered on the crest of the hill. Shank saw the few men from the Shiloh church house. He recognized the twenty-five or so solemn-faced men from Reverend Poe's campground congregation. But there were nine or ten others clustered together whom he'd never seen in Shiloh—hard men with cold eyes and cynical mouths, men with thumbs thrust deep into their belts, men with six guns and rifles.

"Bryan, we didn't ride in here to wait for a Fort Smith marshall." Jud Lewis was red in the face with anger. His white blonde mustache grew down his face like catfish whiskers. "We came to find the killer and give him what he gave. Get out of my way. Come on, boys." The troup of men came down the hill pushing Tom Bryan before them.

Lewis stopped in front of the tent. "Who are you?" he asked Shank.

"Joshua Shank. Who are you?"

Being unrecognized vexed Lewis. "Jud Lewis, acting sheriff of Silam. I'm in charge now." He bent to look inside the tent.

Josh did not step aside. "Just a minute," he said. "The campground belongs to Shiloh."

"Shiloh don't have no sheriff. Silam is the county seat. That makes me the highest authority in the matter."

"Tom Bryan is mayor of Shiloh. He's my authority," Josh said quietly.

"And mine," said Whiting as he and Trimble stepped forward with LeFevre.

"I got a posse here big enough to say different."

"Then put them to work, useful work, instead of tearing up the evidence. We chased someone out of a cave into that big wooded area over the ridge. He probably won't come out of all that cover till nightfall. But we need a lookout up on that ridge." He pointed to a steep rocky hill. "Meanwhile we can make a human circle and close in on him."

Shank looked up Sleepy Creek. Frank Starr and a

small group of Cherokee men were riding in. "We can work together and trap him. We need every man here and more to make that circle."

"Them are Indians," snorted Lewis.

"Jo Belle Walker was Cherokee," said Josh. "They've got an interest in this, too."

"Indians is nothing but filth, setting on prime land while white folks is doin' without. They're the cause of all this. We'd put a stop to 'em if it warn't for you Injun lovers in Shiloh."

Shank ignored Jud Lewis' vitriolic attack on the Indians. "We can all work together and trap the killer or we can fight each other while he gets away. I think the men from Shiloh want him caught, don't you, Tom?"

"Shank's right," said Sam Waters from the crowd. "We can make a circle and trap that devil."

"Sure. Sure. Let's do it," came from the crowd.

"Will your men help, Frank?" Tom Bryan asked the Indian, Frank Starr, who dismounted and stood beside him.

Starr, a mixed blood, had brought Light Horsemen from the Nation. The Light Horse, Indian Police, brought offenders before the tribal court at Tallequah. Many of their prisoners sat in the stone prison there. Experienced lawmen, they were knowledgeable of the territory, fearless before the outlaw. Any crime between Indians within the Nation was in their jurisdiction. Some of them worked closely with Parker's U.S. Deputy Marshalls from Fort Smith to apprehend white renegades who fled to the no-man's land of the Indians.

"We came to help," said Starr. "Maybe our police can help you."

"Help us," snorted Lewis. "Igorant Injuns help us— Ha!"

"Mr. Lewis, perhaps you are right. Some of us have not had the benefits of your fine education, but the Light Horse are experienced in dealing with the criminal element among us," Starr said.

"Well, a Injun probably done it—takes one to find one."

Starr turned to Bryan. "What's the plan, Tom?"

"Closing the circle seems a good idea to me. We can have probably three hundred men here in a couple of hours. They can space out around that thicket and surround whoever's in there."

"Let's go," said Lewis. "I'll put my men over to the west. That way I'll be sure nobody runs to the Injuns' land."

"No. We ought to wait for more men, and all go in at once," said Tom Bryan. "That way we'll be closer together, and there'll be less chance of him slipping between us. We'll send for more help, and they'll come."

Jud Lewis cocked his rifle nervously. "Silam men'll do their waitin' at the thicket."

Starr looked at Shank. "Don't we need to organize ourselves a little? Make some rules, perhaps, to keep from becoming a mob."

"I'd like to see the guns left here," said Shank. "Carrying guns in a closing circle could be dangerous. If we flush him out, there's enough of us to make sure he doesn't get away."

"My men ain't going without their guns," Lewis said.

"Then we'll go without your men," said Bryan. "There are too many of us to take a chance on anybody getting trigger happy and killing someone in the circle."

"No guns. That's fine with us," said Frank Starr.

"Whiskey can't help none neither," Reverend Poe added, looking over the crowd where some of the men were passing a bottle. "Claiming drunkenness for sin don't cut nothing when ye stand before your maker."

"We need to save what evidence we can," Starr suggested. "My men are pretty good at that, if you'll tell us where to look."

"I'll show you," said Shank. He walked with the Light Horse Captain back to the group of Indians who were mingling with Shiloh citizens. "How's Ross Walker and his wife?"

"They're pretty torn up I hear. Can't blame them," said Captain Starr quietly.

Josh shook hands with a couple of the Light Horse. "Good to see you fellas. We need your talent. Nothing like this ever happened in Shiloh before."

The four Indian police nodded, and Josh pointed across the creek toward the cave. "We found the bodies over there."

Together the five walked in the direction he had pointed. Behind them Bryan organized the crowd. The Reverend was hard after the whiskey. Men were beginning to stack guns in one of the women's tents. Coffee boiled in the cook tent, and some of the men were sitting down inside to drink it. The rain slacked into a long cold drizzle, and the men waited.

Shank and the Indians stopped at the body of Jo Belle Walker. He lifted the slicker he'd put over her earlier. The ground was stomped muddy around her by the curious who had come to view the body.

"I ain't let nobody move nothing," said the guard. "But I guess their coming up here musta ruined some of the evidence. Sure is hard on her folks havin' to leave her lay here to be gawked at. Looks like we could do something—maybe take a pitcher for the marshall, and let them take her on home."

"Photographs would save the evidence better than leaving it here in the rain," Starr agreed. "McCurdy, ride into Shiloh and get the photographer."

A young Indian walked quickly back to his horse, mounted and rode away. Josh and the others climbed up the hillside to the overhang where the two other bodies lay.

"What do you suppose he was thinking?" asked Shank. "Killing so mercilessly, then laying the bodies out in neat order like this."

"Maybe the killer didn't put them here, not this way," said the Indian lieutenant. He pointed to a small footprint nearly hidden by brush in the outcropping. "Looks like a woman's boot. Here's a pair of dog tracks, too."

Shank squinted, remembering something he'd seen at the school on his way to Shiloh at dawn. "Could a woman have done it?"

"She might have killed them," Starr answered. "But she couldn't rape them. It's for sure somebody knows a lot more about this than we do. He couldn't have handled three at one time. He must have taken them one at a time and brought them up here. He had to go back, and commit himself to killing three separate times."

"He used the cave around there," Shank said, starting up the trail. Within moments they were looking into the black cave.

"There's the binding twine that was used," said the corporal. "One of the girls had some on her wrist. There are also some clothes here, Captain."

Captain Starr moved to where the young Indian officer kneeled.

"When we were here earlier," Josh said, "We heard a noise back there. We flushed him out of there into the woods. As we crawled through I found this."

He pulled the broken knife from his shirt and handed it to Starr. The Indians studied it.

"Do you have any idea who 'O.M.' might be?" asked the captain as the others watched Josh's face.

"Whiting says 'O.M.'s for Orpheus McKee. I think I saw him with the knife in town once, showing it to some kids at the store."

"It's McKee's knife all right," the lieutenant agreed. "Where'd you find it?"

"In that keyhole crawlway." Shank pointed into the darkness.

"Corporal Hayes, get a lantern and see if there's anything else in there," the captain said.

McCurdy, who had been dispatched for the photographer, stuck his head inside the cave. "Captain, I met the photographer on the road. He's bringing his equipment up to the first body. Ross Walker's acting mean about it."

"Stay here and keep everyone away," the captain commissioned his lieutenant and corporal.

He and Shank began walking back down the hill. He wrapped the broken knife in his handkerchief and put it carefully inside his tunic.

"I wonder who the hell the witness was," he said.

"Whoever it was rang the church bells at Shiloh," Shank answered.

As Shank and Starr walked on in silence, the rain started up hard again. Starr turned up the collar of his tunic, and Shank hunched his shoulders against the stinging rain. Nature herself, irreconcilable, roared and shook against the evil deed of the night and tried to wash the taint of it from the land. Her dark clouds boiled through heavy skies, giving the late morning a feeling of perpetual night. It was almost as if morning had never come, as if time teetered on an endless and evil dawning, a semi-light where nothing was clear and every step was at risk. In that long darkness everything had changed. Three children were dead, three families shattered. A killer had come to Shiloh.

Shank's mind wandered back to what now seemed like a hundred years ago, when he had heard the first sound of the bells.

Shank, Susan and Noah had heard the death bells through the blackness and rain. Until today, death in Shiloh had been a natural part of life. The bells were rung for each death. They always brought sadness and thoughtfulness with their grim message, but never before the horror and fear they would bring on this day.

"It's probably Addie Morrow. She's been growing more feeble all summer," said Susan, her gentle eyes moist and sparkling with unshed tears. "I shall miss her so. She was my first friend in Shiloh." Susan laid the fork by Shank's plate. "The rain would have cooled things off for her, too."

Having finished setting the table in the bright little kitchen, Susan began to roll out dough for the breakfast biscuits. By the time Shank and Noah finished chores she'd have a bountiful breakfast on the table. Susan winced as a crack of lightning sizzled across the black sky and jumped at the percussion of thunder that followed it quickly.

Shank took down his slicker and handed a smaller

one to his boy Noah. "Son, could thee manage chores alone this morning? There's only Lucy to milk and the calf to turn in. Thee knows about the hay and feed for all the critters." The eight-year-old nodded, pleased to be trusted with the morning chores.

"It's too early to ring the bells for a passing," Shank said. "It may not be Addie's died, Susan. On a morning like this it may be something else. I'll see what's going on in Shiloh." Shank opened the kitchen door, paused on the porch, then walked off into the darkness and rain.

In the darkness, the storm tested itself against Shank. His body bent against the strength of it. His eyes blinked and shut as rain struck his hat brim and blew into his face. He wiped the water from his nose and lips. It's like drowning standing up, LeFevre had once said when they had gone hunting as boys. Shank pushed his slicker down as the wind caught beneath and ripped it away from his body. Amid the rain and wind and thunder, he could barely hear the steady drone of the bells.

The path cutting across to Shiloh Road took the run off from the hills, and soon his boots were wet through. At the schoolhouse, Shank stepped onto the small porch and stomped off the wetness. He leaned back out of the force of the driving wind and rain, resting a moment, listening. He thought the bells had stopped.

Shank opened the unlocked door behind him. Rain poured through a hole near the teacher's platform. He lifted the lantern to survey the damage. A tree limb's raw broken edge protruded through the roof. Water covered the floor, slowly seeping between the boards into the mud below. Shank had built this building with his father. In the winter he kept school here. He watched the water coming in and his jaw tightened at the waste and the work to be done, and at the need to hurry on now and leave the ruin.

Lightning rocked the frame building and lit the landscape. Through the tall wide windows of the schoolhouse, Joshua saw a woman standing on the hill above the school. He bent and looked closer. Her cape and hair blew about her in the wind like wings or whipping flames. Her dogs, wet and sullen at her feet, moaned into the rain.

Lightning flashed again. A tree near the road splintered and flamed. When Josh looked back at the hill, the woman was gone. He squinted. Quatie Rose was no illusion, he knew that. He had seen her. And she was gone as suddenly as she came, back to her hermitage above Shiloh.

Shank closed the door behind him as he walked back onto the little stoop. He heard the bells again, louder, more mournful in the sudden quiet of the storm. He glanced swiftly at the hill where Quatie had stood, then walked on toward Shiloh.

Down below by the blackberry thicket, Whiting and another man were trying to restrain Ross Walker. The photographer and his camera lay on the ground, and Walker was kicking at them both.

"You ain't gonna take a pitcher of her like that. You ain't!" he shouted.

"Ross," Shank called his name, and the man's wild gaze looked upon him. "Ross, they don't want to hurt you or Jo Belle. But if you let them take the pictures for evidence against the killer, we can take Jo Belle away, back to town. Let him go, Jon."

Whiting released his grip on the big Indian's arm, but stayed ready for another round if Ross Walker wanted it. The father looked at Josh, his shirt sticking to his body, torn, muddy.

"That your slicker, Shank?" he asked, pointing to the muddy rubber garment. Shank nodded. "The girl's mother and me's grateful for your decency. Take your pitchers so I can get my girl," he turned away.

"I'll bring her to you," Shank said.

In a little while the photographs had been taken, and Shank walked back across Sleepy Creek carrying the slicker-wrapped body of Jo Belle Walker. A farm wagon waited. Shank laid her gently on the rough plank bed. Mrs. Walker's grief came in long deep sobs. Her husband, holding her, tried to stroke comfort into her. But Ross Walker's own eyes were sunken and filled with tears that spilled over and ran down the rough brown cheeks. Grief sat heavily on the man. Whiting and Trimble brought the bodies from the cave. They laid them beside their friend on the wagon floor.

As the small, grim convoy pulled out of the Shiloh campground, Josh saw the first lines of men crossing the creek to form the hunters' circle. Tom Bryan was right, dozens of men had come, were still coming to join. They came in twos, in groups and alone. Indian and white they had come to help. A childkiller drew no man's loyalty. The act was too brutal, too senseless to claim any mercy.

"Where do you suppose they all come from?" asked Walker.

"I don't know," said Shank. "But they all want to help, Ross. Most people want to do what's right. I just hope Tom and Frank Starr can keep it that way. A few mean talkers like Jud Lewis could turn these men into a killing mob."

The rain had stopped when Shank walked out of Sisco's mortuary. The three small bodies and their families were together inside. Shank walked home past the church toward the school. Jo Belle, Mary and Becka had been his students. Opening the door, he saw where each had sat. He walked down the window aisle looking out at the bare dirt playing yard. The hollow worn by the jump rope was full of water. The swings and seesaws were wet and empty. But Josh heard their voices, the soft sweet sound of happy confidences and giggles.

They are dead forever . . . at a murderer's hand. . . .
They have passed from the earth to the place of
long rest, leaving behind anguish for the living . . .
anguish for the living.

Josh thought of Ross Walker's face, tough and hard, yet so vulnerable to pain. He remembered Mrs. Neil twisting in the preacher's arms. "Anguish for the living." Someone had known, had written those words before dawn, before ringing the bells. Someone who knew Cherokee as well as English. He looked back out the window past the play yard at the hill where he had seen Quatie Rose and her dogs in the lightning. The memory of her in the storm's fury, cape and hair blowing wildly in the wind, dissolved into a memory from seven summers before. Quatie had stood in the steaming courtroom box dressed in black, her dark hair pulled into a heavy coil at the back of her neck, blue eyes cold and hard.

"I killed William Bell and shot his son and wife. I have done it," she had said in her soft strong voice.

Quatie Rose was the witness. She had to be. It all fit—the image of her in the schoolhouse window, the woman's boot-print at the cave, the silence of the bells as she made her way to the hill. Quatie Rose knew something of the murders. At the time of her choosing and not before, though angels begged, Quatie would come forth. And Quatie Rose could not lie.

Just before noon, Shank stepped onto his porch at home. Susan opened the door before he could wipe off his boots. She was anxious and her gaze ran quickly over him.

"Oh, Josh, thee's a mess."

Josh looked at himself. He was wet, muddy and dripping on the clean grey painted porch.

"What's happened, Pa? Who died?" said Noah dodging under Susan's arm.

"Let's go inside first, son," Josh said. He leaned on Susan as he caught his heel in the jack, pulling the muddy boots wetly from his soaked feet.

Inside he sat at the table. Susan stirred around, setting coffee and a spoon before him. He looked around the well-ordered kitchen. Pots scoured, scrubbed and shining hung from the ceiling beams. The smell of baking bread came from the oven. There was peace here, the quiet Quakerly order of love.

"Get thy father his robe." Susan sent the boy scurrying as Josh leaned deeply into the chair, comforted by the room and the plain, familiar language of their private world. "Get up, Josh, and strip off those wet things before thee catches cold." She handed him a towel, and he began to wipe his face and head.

"It's bad, Susan, very bad."

He undid his shirt and trousers and tossed them into a pile near the door.

"Come in, son," he said and took the robe. Sitting down he saw his wife and son waiting.

"Last night, at the campground—" he looked at Noah. "Becka Beard, Mary Neil and Jo Belle Walker were killed."

The boy broke across the room to his father, threw his arms about his neck, and began to cry. Susan put her gentle hand on Noah's head, then on Josh's arm. Then she began to pick up the wet clothes and put them on the porch. As she mopped up the mud and water from the floor, Josh heard a little sob.

"Susan," he said, hurt and helpless before her sorrow.

"I am fine, Josh," she sniffled. "Thee must have something to eat. I made bread."

She washed her hands and opened the oven. Steamy heat and the aroma of the crisp round loaves filled the room. She set the loaves and a knife on the table. In a moment she brought butter and strawberry preserves.

"Eat something, Josh," she said, stroking Noah's head.

"Son," Shank said, taking the eight-year-old by his arms and setting him on his knee. "Son, I'm sorry. Sorry it happened. Sorry you have to know. But we believe God has them now. They are not hurt or sad anymore. He knows everything—good or bad. Nothing destroys His plan of love. We believe this. There will be His hand to guide us. Let's go on with life as best we can until we find His way. Now here, try some of thy mother's fresh bread."

He reached across the table and caught Susan's hand. "Father, thank you for the food. Help us to serve you in this season of sorrow. Guide us. Make us your hands to serve. Amen."

"Amen," whispered Susan.

Shank left Susan and Noah at Clary Bryan's to help with the chores of sorrow and drove back to the campground. The little grey mare pulled his rig smartly past the wooden gatepost sign. Shank found Will Le-Fevre sitting with his bound up ankle under the cook tent among the confiscated liquor.

"Hey, Will. How are you feeling?"

"Fine. Just fine," LeFevre grunted. "Look at me, ain't I pretty sitting here while every man in fifteen miles of here is surrounding that no good killin' sonof-abitch."

"You can't help it, besides you did flush him out." The thought seemed to brighten LeFevre. "Say, Will, have you seen Quatie lately?"

LeFevre looked up. "Hell no. You know I ain't seen or spoke to her since before she went to prison. She's been holed up there at Pin Oak since she got back. I tried to see her once and that damn George took a shotgun to me. To hell with her if that's how she feels about it."

"Hm," Josh said. "Guess I'll go see if I can help at the thicket."

LeFevre pulled the cork from a jug of whiskey as Shank started to leave.

"Say Shank, how can you believe in a God who'd let something like this happen to innocent little children?"

"I agreed to follow Him in faith, Will, not to change sides every time He does something or allows something I don't understand. I agreed to stick, to hold off my own judgment. That's all, Will. I'm waiting to understand, too."

From the top of the hill Shank saw that the men had formed a circle around the huge thicket where he and Whiting and LeFevre had chased someone during the morning. The Adams' house, white and clean against the wet greenness of the landscape, marked the southern boundary. Shiloh Road ran around to the west, and Sleepy Creek to the east. If the killer crossed any of the natural barriers before dark, the lookouts would see him easily even before the circle was formed. The thicket was a natural sanctuary full of thick under-growth, ravines and caves.

"He's still in there," Trimble said. "You all close the circle easy and tight, Josh."

Men were spacing themselves apart around the thicket, loafing together, trying to stay dry, waiting for the orders to move in. Shank saw Captain Starr on horseback over to his left. He and Tom Bryan were coordinating the move from the saddle.

"Howdy, Shank," Sam Waters said. "You get 'em all back to Sisco's?" Josh nodded. "Boy, ain't this some deal? Ain't it some deal?"

"Bad as I ever heard," Shank answered.

"Anyhow we know we're looking for that damn no good Orpheus!"

The news was out, Shank thought. Looking about him, he recognized most of the men as Shiloh citizens, men who counted on the town for their business and supply needs. Several of the men were Cherokee, some the full-bloods who dominated the hills to the west. Most of the people around Shiloh had Indian blood or Indian family. The town had grown up just after the relocation of the whole Cherokee nation from Georgia. Men like Tom Bryan and Josh's father had not approved the government's policy. They felt the Cherokee had been moved on a false treaty. As men of conscience they had come along the Trail of Tears to help and settle near their Cherokee friends. That was more than forty years ago. A lot of blood had mixed in those years, but some of the Old Settlers, the Cherokee who had voluntarily left Georgia for Arkansas before being forced out, still refused to mix with the whites or with the heavily mixed newcomers. The fact that so many full-bloods were among the hunters showed the strength of feeling against the killer. Shank smiled a little. There was a community here after all.

Shank's eyes ran over the faces, stopping at the familiar erect form of the Adeyaheh, the creator of spells for the full-bloods. The Adeyaheh held tightly to the old ways. He opposed Shank, as he had opposed Shank's father, in the Shiloh school. Unlike the mixed bloods, he refused to learn white men's ways. He and his followers still held to the old blood laws and kept the Cherokee Council and the Light Horse busy with their secret ceremonies and clan killings.

"Adeyaheh," Shank spoke in Cherokee to the leathery old conjurer who covered his white head with a blanket from the rain. "It is a sad time, but I am pleased to see you looking well."

The old man looked at Shank and nodded.

"Ready, men," called Frank Starr. "Get to your places."

Men moved from under the sheltering trees. They filed down the muddy road, dropping off every ten paces. Josh could hear Tom Bryan's voice shouting instructions to men along the creek. Many of the men had fought in the War and were used to discipline and commands. The Adeyaheh watched his Indians mingle with the other hunters in the circle. Drawing up his blanket, he walked through the tall grass toward the creek to find a place in the ring.

Twice Frank Starr rode up and down the line, checking. Sitting on his eager horse he looked at his watch. At last, he stood in his stirrups. "Ready. All right, men, let's move."

The men stepped off. Some of them ran sticks before and around them in the grass, checking lest the killer belly down in the cover. They moved slowly, a few steps at a time, looking from side to side, keeping the men on either side in measured distance. The rain came up heavier again. A wind drove the cold into the men. Step by step, sometimes yelling to each other, but mostly silent, they advanced toward the center of the thicket.

Starr rode by slowly now, his horse struggling with the terrain. "Good, men, steady on," he said.

Shank stumbled on the rough rocks that covered the land west of Shiloh. He heard an oath from the man next to him. He was caught in a blackberry-wild rose thicket. The thorny branches grabbed his clothes and hair. Jerking away his hands, he tore the flesh.

Shank drew his watch from his pocket and looked at it. They had only crossed the flat land. "This is too slow," he thought. "Two hours to cover a few hundred yards."

"Rest, men," Starr shouted. "Stand or sit where you are. The women will bring you coffee."

Josh turned, stretching his long back. The Shiloh Road was filled with girls and women with parasols, carrying coffee from the farm wagons. Clary Bryan could organize the churchwomen into immediate service. Sometimes folks laughed at the Methodists and their dedication to comforting, their penchant for improving the human condition. But they always took the services.

At the store one day, Shank recalled, Clary had passed him in a huff. "What's up?" he had asked Tom.

"The Methodist women are getting up a bake sale to buy fans for Hell," Bryan had grumped.

"Thank God for Clary," Shank now thought. He saw Susan on the wagon filling pots for the servers. He drank the coffee when it came, squatting, wishing the ground was not too wet to sit on. Bryan and Starr gathered near the creek and sat on their horses talking. Before long a boy collected Shank's cup, and he stood up. The coffee had helped. His insides were warm again.

Starr cantered slowly across the field. "Let's move, men."

The blackjack oak and scrub brush grew thicker as the men advanced up and into the sanctuary. They stooped and dodged the branches, but the verdant limbs tangled them, worried them, compounding the difficulty of their task. The rain was steady and cold and never let up. There was no stopping, no more rest, no more time for hot coffee. Step by step they were coming closer together, closing the living circle around the marauder. For any man to leave now could mean McKee's escape. They climbed up until their legs were weary.

The sky grew darker and Frank Starr checked his watch—six o'clock. The day was slipping from them. "Hurry, hurry," he thought. "We can't lose him now.

Not this close." Aloud he said, "Come on, men. It's not much further."

Josh could see Tom Bryan now. His men were moving steadily. Even the Adeyaheh was moving apace. The old man had been a renowned hunter in his youth. He still carried himself erect.

In front of him Josh saw the top of the hill—another hundred yards and the circle would be closed. He could almost touch the men to his right and left. Along the line, men's faces were taut. Silent, they listened, ready for any noise that might reveal movement. Would McKee pick one of them to break over in his run to escape? Where was he? The thoughts stimulated their senses.

Josh pushed himself between the saplings. The rough bark was wet beneath his hand. Starr's horse stumbled in the rocks. Tying him, the Cherokee walked into the line beside Josh. The circle closed tighter. Closer together the men moved faster, even in the rocks and brush. At last they faced each other across fifty feet of broom grass.

"Come with me, Shank," said Starr. "We'll walk him out."

He and Josh walked into the closing circle, cutting across it, walking up and down. They covered it again and again while the men waited. Josh's mouth felt dry and hard. He looked at the faces of men on the edge. Tom Bryan looked old and tired. He wiped his mustache in a nervous gesture.

"He ain't in there! He ain't here!" yelled Jud Lewis. "Some goddamn Injun let him through!"

Chapter Three

Orpheus McKee lay on his belly in the fox's den, surrounded by the animal stench and the smell of his own fear. All afternoon he lay there, listening to the angry shouts of the hunters. From the darkness of the burrow, he saw the muddy boots of men passing. He held his breath, fearful the sound of it or of his beating heart would alert the men who stopped before the hole to his presence.

Once the boots stopped a long time as the men talked, hunkering on the hillside, drinking coffee to warm their chill. At last, he had to breathe and hid his mouth against the dirt to cover the sound. He pressed himself tight against the earth and prayed not to be found. Not to be found. He did not know why he feared it so much.

He did not remember doing wrong, but his heart was sick within him. It bothered Orpheus that he did not remember. As he waited he tried to remember, tried to find the missing pieces of memory. He had gone to the campmeeting with his sister. He had not liked the skinny white preacher, and he had gone away to the cave. There he sought his hidden bottle, and he got drunk, very drunk because the bottle was full. More he could not remember. He was drunk. That was all. He must have gone to sleep in the crawlway. He must have fallen asleep because he was drunk.

He never hurt anyone before when he was drunk, he thought. The full-blood men had tied him up once when he was very drunk at Ellen Littleowl's wedding and wanted to fight the groom. They had tied him up hand and foot and left him in the cool meadow grass all night. He had gone to sleep there listening to the quiet sounds of crickets and Sleepy Creek with tears flowing silently from his swollen eyes. He never hurt anyone before.

Then, moccasined feet stood before the hole. A claw-like hand dropped a pouch of parched corn, and a foot shoved it into the den and walked on. The gods had heard. They had sent their minister, the Adeyaheh, to him.

Orpheus ate and waited for dark, waited for the boots to stumble past the hole as the search was abandoned, waited for the thicket to grow quiet and then, to teem with its secret life. Orpheus could wait.

Finally, he was running. The sound of his breathing thick and painful, filled ears already deafened by blood churning through his body. And Orpheus ran. Ran against the thick night. Ran against the rain. Ran against the rushing water that filled his moccasins and splashed against his thighs. Ran against the fear of what lay behind him in the darkness. Orpheus McKee would never stop running.

During the night he crossed and re-crossed his trail a dozen times or more. He ran, but he did not know where. Running to the Nation would put him in jeopardy of the Light Horse. Their justice was swift and hard. He had seen their work. His cousin had run into Indian justice. After the quick trial, a consideration of evidence and testimony, the police walked him into a sycamore grove, tied him hand and foot, blindfolded him, pinned a red paper heart over his own living, beating one and shot him. The Light Horse rode away. The family buried him. Light Horse justice could be fast, faster than a running man, faster than his thoughts of escape.

Even if he escaped the Light Horse, the U.S. Deputies from Fort Smith would take him from the Nation to the hell on the border jail under Parker's court. There a hundred or more men crowded into each of the two subterranean holes to lay on the seeping wet stones, waiting for the slow inexorable wheels of justice to grind them into nothingness.

He could see the lights of Shiloh, thin yellow beams from kitchens and parlors where families discussed the gruesome and hopeless events of the day. He saw the lights in the basement of Sisco's Mortuary burning late.

He saw the lights of lonely farmhouses where dogs slept by the door and men kept their long guns loaded and at hand. He saw the lights of his sister Minnie's house, saw them go out like her hope for him. He saw the warmth of those lights and felt his loneliness, his exile. He ran harder, trying to think but losing the thoughts as he stumbled against the night tangles of root, rocks, branches and trees. Tangles that a man so easily steps over in the daylight.

Orpheus McKee fell to the earth. He tripped, fell to his knees, then stretched full length on the muddy ground. He decided to die. The thought of dying intrigued him, filled him with ease. A little while and he would do it, reach into his belt for the charmed knife. He felt for the knife and did not find it. He sat up, searching his body for it. Someone had robbed him, taken his hope.

"What are you looking for?" He heard the chilling words above him. "What do you look for, I said?" The figure was tall, sparse like the winter trees.

"My knife. I've lost my knife," Orpheus said as the figure bent over him.

"The laws have your knife," the voice said as boney fingers searched his arm for the joining with the body and pulled him to his feet. "You, Orpheus McKee, come with me. Get up, Cherokee brother."

Death, he thought, had come for him after all. He was safe now in its shadow. It was not so bad, this death. He was no worse off. And he was not alone any more.

Judson Lewis jammed his foot against the door to Minnie McKee's frame shanty. The unlocked door splintered around his leg, and he hopped to draw it out. Across the room, Minnie held her children to her as the Silam posse took over the room. The men scattered across the bare floor, kicking chairs, scattering dishes and clothes, overturning anything in their way, careless of the destruction.

"Goddamn stink of hominy," said Lewis. "Look in there, Herb." He gestured his deputy toward a lean-to room hidden behind a blanket door. Herb Latta and his men gripped their guns tighter, eased back the blanket, and went inside.

"He ain't here," Latta called out. "But I got his good shirt."

Lewis surveyed the dark room where he stood. Finally his eyes rested on the Indian woman and her children. "Where's McKee?"

Minnie did not answer but drew her children closer, holding them by their heads and covering their ears with her trembling fingers.

"I said, where's your brother?" Lewis raised his voice. "Is this here his shirt?" He waved the ragged garment before her.

Minnie McKee was not deaf, nor was she slow-witted. She understood the English words. She knew what Jud Lewis and the Silam thugs wanted. But she watched him stoically, showing no sign that she understood.

The Shiloh Cherokee knew the situation. The full-bloods had talked together yesterday. If Orpheus had done the killing, they had said, they would give him to the Light Horse, or better, to Ross Walker. He was not their people to do such killing. The old law, the blood law before the written Cherokee constitution, required blood for blood. No circumstance mitigated the taking of the life for the life. If Orpheus had killed the children, he was a dead man. Nothing but innocence could save him from the Cherokee. His life belonged to Ross Walker, to the Walker clan.

Minnie knew Orpheus had shamed his family by running. In the old times, Ross Walker would have killed someone of the McKees, perhaps one of Minnie's clan. And the people would have accepted this as justice. Minnie would have accepted the justice, for Orpheus was her blood. The family would pay the price of their relation and the shame it brought. They believed this was right. By running Orpheus would suffer more than if he had taken the death road himself. He would suffer for his killing guilt and for the pain and shame he brought to his family. To suffer personally was nothing, but to bring death by your sin to a loved one was Cherokee hell. Minnie knew this.

She knew Orpheus did not return for some reason beyond guilt.

Minnie knew Ross Walker was a mixed blood, a believer in written laws, not laws of guilt. Ross Walker would not come to kill Orpheus or one of their clan. But these whites who cared nothing for the honor of guilt would kill Orpheus swiftly if they caught him. They would not consider his guilt. They would kill him because he was an Indian, because of their own fear and hate—fear of what they did not understand and hate that grew from their hunger for the Indian land.

The white man considered land to be almost like his other self. Land was himself—something to guard, protect, defend tenaciously against other men. Only when he possessed land did he have worth. He was free in his world only when he owned the land. To the Indian, the earth was free, and he lived by her permission, grateful and generous in his turn. He could claim only what he could use. That was his way. He could set down roots anywhere in the Nation and use as much land as he wanted to work. For such a system to work required honor and respect and community. The white men did not have this. They did not trust each other because they knew their own hearts. That is what Minnie thought as she looked at the intruders encircling her.

She had seen men like these before. She had seen them on the roads with their pale thin wives and hollow-eyed children as the Washington soldiers rounded them up and drove them from the Indian territory. She had seen them farming Indian land for the mixed bloods, like Quatie Rose and Frank Starr, who got them working permits. Using the white laborers the rich Cherokee claimed acres they could not work themselves and turned profits that paid for fine educations and silk clothes and brick houses and shining carriages and sleek blooded horses. She had seen these white men before. She had seen the land hunger and Indian hate in them.

"That's his shirt a'right," one of the Shiloh men said. "I seen him wear it."

"Where's your brother?" Jud Lewis said again. "Goddamn stupid connuche eater Injun," he said to the men with him. "Injuns ain't human. Can't get nothing through their thick heads. Look at them fat stupid faces, ain't no intelligence in their eyes, just blank stares, like animals. But them government bastards want 'em treated like people, better'n white folks." Lewis studied the Indian woman kneeling in the ragged unmade bed, holding her children. "Look under the bed, Herb."

Latta followed the order, looked and ran his gun under the iron bed frame. His hand rested on the shuck mattress as he kneeled. When he stood again, he wiped it broadly on his pants and spit a stream of tobacco into the floor, showing Minnie and the children his contempt.

"Let's go, then," Lewis said, turning toward the door. "I can't stand this here stink no longer."

"This stink," Minnie's smallest child repeated before the Indian woman could stop her.

Lewis looked back. "What say, gnit?" But the child had withdrawn again into the silent world of the Cherokee. "Let's go," he said, following his men back across the room. At the door he bumped against the overturned table and angrily threw it through the window. Where it had been was a book. He stooped, studying the open and well-worn pages of McGuffey's Fifth Reader:

Whither are the Cherokee to go? What are the benefits of the change? What system has been matured for their security? What laws for their government? These questions are answered only by gilded promises in general terms; they are to become enlightened and civilized husbandmen. They now live by the cultivation of the soil and the mechanical arts. It is proposed to send them from their cotton fields, their farms and their gardens, to a distant and unsubdued wilderness; to make them tillers of the earth; to remove them from their looms, their workshops, their printing press, their schools and churches, near the white settlements, to frowning forests, surrounded by naked savages, that they may become enlightened and civilized.

Lewis kicked the book across the room into a corner. "Bunk! Goddamn Quaker schoolteacher Shank," he said stepping out into the bright morning sun.

Herb Latta and the others were studying the shirt in the light.

"Ain't no blood on it," someone said. "No blood atall."

"No, but she'll sure give the dogs a whiff," Latta said, holding the shirt away from him. "Ain't that right, Jud?"

Lewis nodded and grunted, but he was not listening. He walked on back toward his horse, and the others slowly followed. He was thinking about Joshua Shank.

"Hey, Herb," he said riding back. "What do you know about this Shank fella?"

"He ain't nothing to worry about. He's a Quaker. Don't believe in fightin'. Can't lift a finger 'cause of his religion, that there still small voice a tellin' him to love his fellerman and do 'em good not harm. It's their way to find good in everybody. Ain't practical far as I can see. Man, this world'll eat a man alive that believes that."

"Yeah," said Lewis without emotion. "He won't fight cause of his religion? But the Injuns likes him, don't they?"

"Ought to. His old man come from Georgie with them when Andy Jackson refused to protect 'em. The whole damn family has been a schoolin' them and a carryin' them to them Injun schools up north ever since. Shiloh folks say Shank don't even know any more they're Injuns. They also resents his marrying that outlander Pennsylvania woman when there was fine womenfolk here. Say she's some kind of preacher. Damn. Think of what kind of man would marry a preachin' woman. Jesus. And let her go on a doin' it, too. Way I see it a man fights for what he believes in and don't let no woman get too big for her britches. Shank can't have no character."

Lewis drove his spurs into his startled horse and galloped toward town.

The rain stopped during the night, and the late-summer sun lit the fresh greenness with an eye-squinting brightness. Jaybirds screeched thanksgiving through the trees as other birds chatted among themselves about the rain. Rivulets ran their last drops through the grass. The streams cleared away to their bright rocky bottoms. The air smelled wet and clean as Shank stood on his porch sipping coffee, leaning against a post. His animals had passed the storm in the tight new barn. A few hours and he would release them to the pastures. Noah came out of the small side door of the creamery carrying the sloshing milk bucket with both hands on the bail.

"He's still so small," said Susan.

"He wanted to bring it in alone, Susan."

"I know, I know. But sometimes I want more than I can carry, and I'm not eight years old."

Shank reached down the steps and caught the pail. His large brown hand wrapped around the rough stubby fingers of his son.

"Thanks, Pa," the boy said, struggling up the steps one muddy rubber boot at a time.

Josh put his arm around Noah and kissed the top of his towhead. The boy and Susan were his life. Without her and the boy, he wouldn't care much about anything. He wouldn't care about building the farm just for himself. He wouldn't care so much about the school, about the town, for they wouldn't be his in the same way. The family gave meaning to the man. Without them his heart would be empty and nothing would matter too much. Without them he'd be a floater, a hired hand working for roof and food and a little tobacco money. Without them, he thought, like the families of the girls killed at the campground. So swiftly and finally their families were without them.

Susan was now sweeping the porch. "Leave thy work and come see the morning," Shank said. And the man and the woman and the child stood together on the grey painted porch listening to the birds' songs in the clear fresh morning air. "I love thee both," he said softly. "I love thee."

And the small voice inside him said, "How much, Josh? Enough to fight, to kill? Enough to keep thy faith and theirs?"

After breakfast Shank saddled the mare and rode into Shiloh. The main street was a muddy mire from the wagons and teams of yesterday and this morning.

"Get down, Josh," Frank Sims the barber said as Josh rode up to the hitch rail. "Good to see the sun, ain't it. My bones even feel better."

"Mine, too," said Shank, tying the mare to the rail.

"Lyin', thievin' damn Injun," Shank heard the words come from Bryan's General Store and looked up.

"That's been going on since first light. Tom let some of that bunch from Silam sleep in the church. Naturally the first thing they thought of after their free breakfast was Indians and them letting Orpheus go."

"Maybe they ain't so wrong as you think," Sam Waters said from the porch. We had him six ways to Sunday and then he was gone."

"Sam, you know better. None of the men in the circle wanted the killer to escape," Shank said, walking up the steps.

"Blood's thicker than water," Sam replied. Several of the men around him nodded agreement. "We let Starr and them Indian police big dog around here yesterday and came up empty. Something sure as hell happened."

"Maybe LeFevre, Whiting and I took too long getting back, and he got away then. Maybe he never was in there, Sam. Did you ever think of that? Maybe it was our own fault for being so slow."

"He was there." Sam's voice was rigid, set like his jaw.

Shank walked the sunlit boards to the store. Jud

Lewis sat on a flour barrel flapping a piece of paper. Other men from Shiloh and Silam crowded the room, but no one was buying anything.

"Marshall ain't coming for a week. Ain't clearly his jurisdiction. Got to know the killer went to the Nations, that he's a Injun. Well, I'll tell you whose jurisdiction it is. It's mine. And Orpheus McKee is a Injun, and if he's on this side of the line or close to it, he's gonna be a good Injun." Lewis laughed and the men around him laughed at the frontier joke of a good Indian being a dead Indian. "My dog man'll be here before noon, and we'll get to sniffing out that red bastard."

Shank leaned against the broad doorway.

"Rained last night, Lewis," he said. "Don't you think maybe the dogs will have a time finding any trail?"

"Well, schoolteacher, famous tracker, we got this from McKee's sister." Lewis held up the faded flannel shirt. "This plus a little find made by some boys from Silam ought to put the dogs on him."

"Did she give you the shirt?"

"Didn't ask her to, just went in his room and took it. Now if your boys would get up early like mine you might find yourselves a little lean-to cave with a fire hole still hot and canned beans simmering. It ain't rainin' now, Shank, and we're goin' after the killer as soon as the dogs get here. Unless, of course, you wants to loan us that fine brace of yours."

Tom Bryan put his hand on Shank's shoulder. "Don't let him push you, Josh. Your dogs are not man hunters."

"Will you leave your guns here and agree to bring Orpheus in for a fair trial?" Shank asked.

"Ain't you fine, nasty nice, too. We're gonna save everybody a lot of expense and trouble. You gonna bring your dogs or no?"

"No. I'll not set my dogs on a man to be killed without a fair trial. We might just be wrong about Orpheus."

"He didn't give those little girls no fair trial," Lewis shouted. The men in the store agreed in loud voices.

Shank shoved past Sims and Waters and the others

who clustered around the door. "Damn schoolteacher," he heard someone say. Outside, Tom Bryan caught up to Shank.

"What's this about a lean-to cave?" Shank asked.

"Adams drove his cows out this morning. Took a stort cut home and found a fire and food. He told the men sleeping at the church, and they're sure the fire was Orpheus'. Anyhow they went over to his sister's, broke in, scared her and her kids half to death."

"Where's Starr and the Light Horse?"

"They've decided not to mix in here anymore after yesterday. The Light Horse are looking for McKee in the Nations."

"The marshall?"

"Most of them are away from Fort Smith. Unless we can prove McKee did it and went to the Nations, they can't enter anyway. The Fifth District only covers crimes that are on Federal lands or in Indian country."

"What time is the funeral?" Shank asked, unhitching the grey.

"Ten o'clock," answered Bryan as Shank mounted and rode toward home.

The Baptist, Methodist Church and Masonic Hall was an imposing white frame structure surrounded on three sides by verdant trees, a sparse lawn and wagon yard, and on the fourth a hill rolled softly down into Sleepy Creek. The three-storied building accommodated two churches every Sunday, the women's societies during the week and the men's lodge at regular intervals.

It was the essence of the town, incorporating individual preference and community spirit. In some flash of genius the city fathers had seen both the economic and civic values of combining their resources. Everyone in Shiloh found satisfaction in some activity there, and since they met together, or nearly so, the town mixed easily before and after the featured events.

Singing was at times difficult. The Baptists by numbers were the best singers. But the sequential hymns, alternating across a Sunday morning, gave a sense of fullness to the grove. Those in counterpoint gave the merry air of a round. There was a wholesome competitiveness as song leaders matched hallelujahs.

Shank put his arm around Susan's waist as he guided Noah down the wide center aisle behind the two tiny coffins.

"Looks like Ross Walker would have wanted his girl with the others," said Pettigrew Wills. "They were friends, all of 'em went to Sunday school together. Why, Ross and his missus was members here."

"Walker's decided he's an Indian today, that's for sure," Josh heard Jim Taylor's deep voice behind him.

At the top of the porch stair Shank paused and put on his broad brimmed hat. He saw the caskets and families leading off toward the burying ground. The men from Shiloh were beginning to gather in the yard beneath the broad oak.

"You and Noah go on to the cemetery," he said, leaving his family for the group beneath the tree.

"When's that dog man comin'?" Pettigrew Wills asked.

"Before noon," said Tom Bryan, opening the face of his old gold watch. "Looks like the Silam bunch are going to get their chance to run things awhile."

"They're runnin' things now. There wasn't a Cherokee in church today," Shank said.

"Oh, they are busy burying their own," said Serge McGuire.

"We've buried our dead together for forty years," Tom Bryan said. "After yesterday, our Cherokee friends don't feel welcome here, and our enemies are calling the tune."

"Well," Sam Waters said, "An Indian could've let McKee through."

"So could a white man. Anyone in the circle could have missed him," said Shank. "Or maybe he wasn't even there."

"Circle was your idea, Shank," Waters said. "You said he was in the thicket. You said to make a circle."

"I've been wrong before," Shank answered.

Tom Bryan rejoined the talk. "The bunch from

Silam is running over what we've built up. All they want is to get rid of the Cherokee and get their land."

"A lot of them Indians *is* settin' on good land and not using it," McGuire said.

"Ain't we been through this before?" LeFevre said, coming around the tree. He was clean and fresh shaven. But he was noticeably pale. "Anytime Indians have what we want they're dangerous, lazy, no-good bastards. I'm surprised at you boys, you act like you believe that. You and I both know that's just what we tell ourselves to get the courage to do something that's wrong. Damn," he said unscrewing the cap from a pint bottle of whiskey.

"Dog man's here!" someone shouted from down the street. The men moved off toward the store.

"Lots of folks are thinking thoughts they never considered before," Shank said to LeFevre.

"Bet our side loses," LeFevre said.

"Oh, Will. Come on, let's see these dogs."

"I got dogs. You got dogs. Quatie's got dogs. But there ain't no dogs like these dogs."

The wagon bed contained a rough unpainted cedar box. Holes were drilled for air. A dirty door with a locked hasp secured the contents. Men in the street and on the store porch stretched to see the box, then turned to the dog man.

Hosea Wilkins wore a derby hat pulled down securely over the long greasy hair that protruded. He wore galluses over a once red union suit and stuffed his dirt-caked britches in high topped boots with floppy pulls. A week's growth of stubby whiskers covered the lower part of his face.

"Smells like a dog man, don't he?" observed LeFevre as Wilkins spit and shook hot hands with a jubilant Jud Lewis.

"Trot 'em out," yelled LeFevre. "Let's see your goddamn dogs."

Hosea Wilkins and Jud Lewis walked solemnly around to the box as the crowd parted before them. A long dirty leather string tied securely to Wilkins' belt loop held the key. He drew it out of his hip pocket and placed it in the lock. A double thump came from within the box. LeFevre leaned on Josh's shoulder to get the first glimpse of the contents. Wilkins hung the lock carefully back in the loop, snapped it and swung open the door. A mastiff head emerged blinking at the summer sun.

"Hell, that dog ain't got a cold nose. He can't smell worth two hoots in Hell," said LeFevre.

Shank set his jaw and folded his arms as the tailless black and tan mutt emerged.

"This here's my prize, boys," Hosea told the crowd. "Sweetie Cakes, my wife named him, Sweetie Cakes has been treein' everything in Madison County for seven year. He brung in four excapees and three lost chillern. A trophy for ever year. Now he's a gonna get his eighth."

Sweetie Cakes yawned and laid down on the wagon bed. The crowd pondered the sleepy dog.

Hosea turned and reached into the depths of the box, pulling forth a blue tick hound snapping and growling. Men in the front stepped back as the dog revealed the tight row of small teeth and sharp fangs beneath its upper lip.

"Here. Set down, Blue," said Wilkins, snapping a chain into the wide leather collar and gingerly getting away before jerking the dog down. "Yes, sir. He's a mean 'un. Eat your arm off when you try to feed him. Yes, sir."

"Reckon that's why he's so skinny," shouted Le-Fevre. "Wilkins is scared to feed him." Quietly he added, "Jesus, Josh, that man's scared of his own dog." LeFevre left Shank and hobbled to the store porch to sit down.

"Get me that shirt, Herb," Jud Lewis yelled. In a moment Orpheus McKee's old garment was handed through the crowd to the Silam sheriff. Hosea Wilkins soused it under the noses of the dogs. The Blue Tick sniffed short and growled. The black raised his head, obligingly inhaled the garment, blinked and laid the huge head back on his front feet.

"Let's go get him, boys. Make us a path," said Lewis as he led the crowd behind Bryan's store and off toward the campsite Adams had found.

Shank watched for awhile then sat down beside LeFevre. "I've heard of that black dog before," he said. "He's a good one."

"Yeah, but think of yellin' him in on a cold crisp night. 'Sweetie Cakes. Ho, Sweetie Cakes. Sweetie.'" LeFevre grinned and shook his head.

Most of the Shiloh men returned to the store after seeing the dogs take the scent. During the afternoon, Josh watched others returning, from where he worked on the roof of the schoolhouse. He placed the new split shingles and drove the nails expertly into place.

Joshua Shank was a teacher because he believed that ignorance was a great and common evil. Many times on the frontier he had seen men die because of what they did not know. He had seen them live as animals because they could conceive nothing more. He had seen children born in ignorance and trapped by it. Learning, like religion, Josh believed had to go with a man every day, teach him his trade or farming, counsel him in sorrow or decision, entertain him in his leisure. Learning, like religion, could set a man free. Learning was not a dead thing in books. It was alive. A person who could not read and cipher was a cripple. Sometimes he could do civilized things, but people were amazed by the mere execution of the deed rather than the quality of the accomplishment. They took interest like they did in a paralyzed man who managed to paint by holding a brush between his teeth. Josh's students learned at different rates and with different need, but they learned and they went home more independent of the tyranny of ignorance.

From the schoolhouse roof, Josh could see his farm. Susan stood in the yard scattering scraps to the busy chickens. The calf dragged Noah as he tried to teach it to lead.

Shank smiled, looking at his world. Lately he had tended to lean back, contented with what he saw. He was a satisfied man. His home and family were secure. Susan laughed often, brimming over with love and contentment. Noah was quick, strong, growing, and his heart was good and willing. Every year there was

improvement in the farm, like the new barn he had
built last spring. The crops were good, especially the
apple trees. The livestock bore a steady increase.
Shank had not lost a colt, calf or lamb in a dozen
birthing seasons.

The school too was growing. He no longer had to
bribe the full-bloods into coming. They could see for
themselves what education meant to the mixed bloods
and whites, and they wanted the good for themselves.
The Indians trusted him with their children—trusted
him to teach the new ways without ridiculing or destroying the old ways. Josh had friends. Shiloh was full
of good people. He was pleased with his world, confident that his way bore the promised fruit.

But the smile quickly faded when he saw the men at
the store arguing and listening to hot words. A chill
ran through him and he shuddered on the hot summer
day. Maybe he was too confident. Maybe his beliefs
were just untested. Maybe this was the season when he
would struggle to reaffirm or abandon the simple way
of absolute trust and obedience to his God. Shank
considered this. He reddened at the pride he took in
his accomplishments as if he had done everything
alone, as if he were above other men's problems. He
said a quick prayer against his pride and determined to
consider the deceit in his heart in the next quiet time
when he waited silently for God, listening for the still
small voice of divine guidance.

Chapter Four

At last finished with the roof, Shank gathered his tools and climbed down the ladder. Unrolling his sleeves, he walked into town.

Will LeFevre was asleep or passed out on the steps of Bryan's store. Men propped or sat all around the store and barbershop. A sweltering heat had followed the rain. The windows and doors were thrown out wide. But no breeze stirred and the air hung heavy on the men. Dark stains of sweat showed on their backs and under their arms.

"We should have heard something by this time. Them dogs've been running for more 'n four hour," said a skinny man with tobacco stains on his stubby whiskers.

"Whiting said he'd blow when they got close. And he will," Tom Bryan said, fanning himself with a paper fan from Sisco's Funeral Parlor.

On the porch LeFevre wiped his eyes and listened. The sound of the hunting horn came faint and distant across the hot afternoon.

"It's Jon's horn!" he shouted.

The men dashed onto the porch and stood listening.

"By god, they've got him! Let's go help 'em," Red Bowley shouted to his brothers.

"Josh, go make sure he gets in," LeFevre said, grabbing Shank's arm. "They may not hang him if somebody'll make 'em think about the law. Whiting's there. Together you might make 'em see. My horse is around back."

Shank's heart pounded as he followed the Bowleys on their mules across the hills and fields. In a little while Whiting sounded the horn again, and Shank knew where he was. He cut across toward the Devil's Legion, the evil cave-pocked mountain. By the time he'd tied LeFevre's horse, he knew how high up **the** hunters had gone. Scrambling up the steep grade along the narrow path, he heard the men shouting.

In a little while he saw the dogs running, dragging the men who held them. Shank usually liked to watch hounds work a trail, but these dogs hunted a man. It was better to watch the beasts' innocent desire on a long autumn night when their voices rang clearly through the woods, though even that meant a bloody kill in the end.

The dogs had been dragging Lewis and Wilkins faster and faster. The hunters sensed their quarry at hand. Then the blue tick suddenly sat down on its haunches and whined. The black circled back and reworked the trail. It ran back, picked up the scent and ran forward, nose down again. Again it circled. Then ran forward. Then back. Again forward. Again back. The blue tick was shivering, hiding against the rocks, growling soft and low. Hosea jerked the chain but the dog lay back against it. The dog man tried to kick him up, but the dog howled and moved under a shale outcropping.

"Goddamn dog. Heah. Get. Get out!" Hosea barked, pulling on the chain till it cut into his hands and drew blood.

"Look at that," said Whiting, pointing toward Jud Lewis who suddenly held a slack leash. The black mastiff was on its stomach, crawling, then it rolled over on its side. Hosea threw his chain to the near man and ran to the quivering animal. He began to stroke it.

"What the hell's happened here?" said Lewis.

"They lost the scent, that's what's happened," Jon Whiting answered. "The dogs are through. From here on if he's tracked it'll be by us."

"Let's go. He's got to be just up ahead." Lewis motioned the men forward.

The clearing became quiet. Shank walked to the outcropping where the blue tick hound hid. He followed the chain to the collar and unsnapped it. The dog backed into the shadow.

Tears ran down Hosea Wilkins' face as he stroked the black mutt. "He's my wife's pet," he said hoarsely.

"He once saved three lost children. He ain't never quit afore."

Shank kneeled and ran his hand along the dog's slick black side. "Come on," he said, lifting the mastiff into his arms. Hosea glanced toward the blue tick. "Come on. He'll find us."

At the bottom of the hill, Shank lay the black dog in the creek water. He held its head up and rubbed water around the eyes and muzzle.

"It's hot today," he said. "He may have overheated. We'll try to cool him off." The dog man watched, suspended in emotion for the animal. "You take him now," Shank said, lifting the huge head for Wilkins' hand to slide beneath. The dog's eyes opened and darted about at unseen things. He began to pant. "I've got to go back now."

Shank left the old man and his dog and walked back toward the hunters. He walked past where the blue tick hid. He followed the boot tracks till he heard the hunters' voices.

"Ain't no sech thing as a witch," he heard Jud Lewis say. "Don't even say sech igorant Injun crap."

"Well, we've had this Orpheus twice, and he's disappeared into thin air both times," Whiting said. "Cherokees ain't ignorant, and they believe in witches. They try 'em and kill 'em. It ain't human the way he disappears, that's for sure."

The funeral was over. The yard at Ross Walker's farm was full of buggies and horses. Cherokee men sat or stood talking in the shade of oak and maple trees or leaned contemplatively against the shady side of the straight two-story house. Inside, the women were comforting Mrs. Walker. Down along Sleepy Creek the children chased crawdads on the rocky bottom beneath the cold clear water.

Ross Walker was a mixed blood, more white than red. Like many whose parents had come over the Trail of Tears, he did not remember Georgia or the old ways. His life had been spent here, making a home for his wife and children, daily building a secure life on

industry and determination. He sat now in the swing he
had ordered for his wife's birthday.

"You trust children will live beyond you. You count
on them going on. To have her dead, killed ..." His
words trailed off, and he dropped his head, thinking
thoughts he could not say. "Damn Orpheus. Damn
him to hell," he finally said.

Frank Starr sat with his feet propped on a stump.
He suddenly moved them and let his chair legs thump
down on the clipped green grass.

"The Light Horse are searching for him, Ross.
They'll hunt him out if he's this side of the line. And
they've got dogs coming into Shiloh to follow the trail
they found this morning. Between us we will find him,"
Starr said.

"Orpheus is a woodsman," the Adeyaheh spoke
softly as he moved into the group. "He follows the old
gods, and they protect him."

The Adeyaheh had come to Walker's in spite of
their Christian funeral service. The old conjurer had
stayed behind the crowd and chanted over the grave,
sanctifying it against the foreign god and the evil spirit
of the witch. Walker had watched, but he did not run
the old man off. In other times he had hated the
Adeyaheh with his spells and incantations and suspicions of all that was white. But seeing the old man
today over his daughter's grave had reassured him in
some way he could not describe.

"He killed Jo Belle. What spirit protects a child
killer?" asked Starr.

"Evil ones. Evil gods. Witches," said the Adeyaheh.

"Well, they had better work hard for this is a new
time. Men are stronger and wiser," Starr said. "We
don't fool ourselves with superstitions. We act on fact
and rely on new skills and better ways."

"They hear you, Frank Starr," the old man whispered venomously. "They know you live in a white
man's house and use his easy ways. The old ones are
angry and wait to show their power. They may have a
lesson for you and your friends."

"That almost sounds like a threat, doesn't it?" said
Starr. "It would be a great victory for you if the old

ones could be resurrected. But I tell you, there are no old ones. There is no mystery, no power but that of men and the learning they bring to every task. We'll find Orpheus, no matter how the old gods hide him. We'll find him and we'll try him for his crime."

"Try him? You or the whites? Do they not seek him for their justice?" asked the Adeyaheh.

"Whoever catches him first will try him," answered Starr. "He can't die but once, but both will be satisfied."

"What if he did not do the crime? What if we discover this? Will the whites accept this?"

"They might retry him, but if he's innocent he's innocent. They'll want to make sure he's the right man. Nobody wants to think about killing the wrong man and letting a killer roam around," Starr said.

"When was a Cherokee ever innocent before a white court?" asked the Adeyaheh.

"Arguing with you is like spitting in the wind," Starr said standing up. "The facts don't bother you a bit, if you can see a chance to play on foolish minds. We have to have some faith in our neighbors. Shiloh has always been a good town for Indians and whites. They are our friends."

"Friends? Your white Jesus says a friend lays down his life for others. Will Shiloh be your friends when they count the cost? Will one man even be your friend?"

The lights in Tom Bryan's store meant the men were still in town. The Bowley brothers' mules slept at the rail. LeFevre wasn't around, and Shank went inside to look for him. Shank scanned the room for LeFevre, but he wasn't there.

Gail Bowley sat on the counter by the coffee grinder.

"It was not natural. Two dogs hot on the scent and then one quit and t'other passed out. Couldn't happen, no sir. Not twice without some unnatural help," he said to his audience.

"Are you sayin' you believe in haintes, Gail?" Sims the barber joked.

"I'm sayin' it ain't natural. The killings weren't natural and the disappearing weren't natural. Besides, the Cherokee believes in witches. They've knowed Arkansas a lot longer than we have. You got to give 'em that."

"I'd give 'em a lot more," said Herb Latta, Jud Lewis' deputy. "If the killin' and disappearin' ain't natural, it's because no white man done it. It ain't our way. Them Cherokees for all their fine clothes and airs is savages, animals—gut-eatin' animals."

George, Quatie Rose's hired man, leaned in the back doorway waiting for Tom Bryan to fill his grocery order. He looked out the door into the night, his back to the room, but Shank knew, from the slight turn of his head, the black man was listening.

"Shut up," Bryan said suddenly to Latta.

The others looked at the storekeeper, unfamiliar with the tone of his voice. Then they followed his gaze to the front door. Frank Starr, Ross Walker and two other Indians stood in the entrance.

"Come in. Come on in. There's nothing in here but a bunch of hot air," Tom Bryan said.

"The hell they will come in," Herb Latta shouted and jumped from his box. He was a small man with a banty rooster disposition and strut. "Shiloh's under martial law. No Injuns in town after sundown. Show 'em out, boys."

"Hold on," Bryan protested. "This is my store, and these are my friends."

"Your store's in Shiloh. And Shiloh's under the law of Sheriff Judson Lewis. He set the curfew this morning."

"You can't declare martial law here without our vote, without our council's vote," Bryan said.

"Be quiet, Tom," said Asa Hardcastle. "We voted this morning while you was in church. We knowed how you felt about Injuns, but the majority of us believe it's time we stood up for our own selves. Times have changed, Tom. Shiloh's changed."

"My god, Asa, Ross's girl was killed out there same as the white girls," Tom Bryan said, dropping his head.

Herb Latta smirked. "Show 'em out, boys. If you

savages got money to spend here, spend it before sundown. Now git!"

Shank looked at Tom, his confidence shaken, his head bowed. He looked at the men of Shiloh mixed now with the Silam intruders. He saw no friend. Men he knew watched silently as the thugs walked toward the four Indians. The same chill he had felt that afternoon ran through him. Joshua Shank stepped in front of the advancing bullies.

"These men came in peace," he said. "And they'll leave that way when they've had their say."

The Cherokee were a nation of orators, accustomed to fighting injustice with law and reason, but they set their jaws ready for the first hand to fall upon them.

"You see it is no use to work with the whites," the voice of the Adeyaheh said in Cherokee as he stepped from the shadows behind the four. "I told you not to come. These white men do not love us. We are alone. We must separate ourselves from them."

The old man pulled his robe tighter about him and walked into the night. Shank watched the four turn and follow him into the darkness. He stepped onto the porch where the damp coolness from Sleepy Creek had finally come. He could hear the voices of the men behind him above the stillness of the night and the cricket sounds.

"Bet our side loses," LeFevre said from the corner.

"The hell we will," Joshua Shank said, his square jaw set.

Chapter Five

Orpheus McKee sipped thick black coffee before the fireplace in the Adeyaheh's secret medicine hut. Steam filled his nostrils, and he felt clearheaded for the first time in two days.

First there had been the frenzied campmeeting full of fire and fear and white man's godways.

"Repent! Repent now! For the fires of hell are upon you," Preacher Poe had thrust his thick Bible into the air. The campfires played on his angular features, creating a grotesque mask before Orpheus' eyes. And suddenly, the black clad preacher leaped from the log platform and strode down the wide aisle between the pew benches. His large hands fell on shoulders in the congregation, and he hurled men to the ground in the power of his words.

"On your knees, sinner. God Almighty sees your black and callous hearts. He hears the sweet words of your lips hiding the blackness within you. He wants to save you from the flesh and the fire, but ye got to come to him and repent. Or he'll have to burn ye in hell's fire forever. Feel the heat a risin' around you. Nothin' but flame as far as yer burnin' eyes can see. And yer craving a drop a' water.

" 'Oh, jest a cup to quench my thirst,' ye begs.

"And Satan smiles sweetly his gleamin' teeth dancin' with the fire's light, and he hands ye a cup of burning fire to drink. Taste the liquid fire a running down your poor parched throat and Repent!"

Beside him, Orpheus' sister Minnie fell forward, her arms and shoulders weaving over the ground. "Save my brother, Preacher. Save my baby brother. He is a good man, but he don't believe."

"Amen. Amen." Orpheus heard the people say.

And Poe grabbed Orpheus' head in his hands. Holding the Holy Bible still, he pressed it and his knuckles against Orpheus' ear. "Are ye afeared of hell-fire, brother?"

Orpheus was afraid of hell, afraid of everlasting fire and tormented souls separated forever from the creator of acorns and oak trees, of rippling brooks running between snow banks, of larks' songs and of the other treasures of Orpheus' world. He had sat and listened and the fear of unrelieved flame caused him to tremble, and then to shake, and finally with the preacher's fist upon him, to jump to his feet yelling,

"Jesus. Jesus. Save me, Jesus."

Afraid, ashamed of the fear and his betrayal of the Cherokee gods, Orpheus had run into the darkness, out into the woods, into the cool air, and up the hill and into the cave. To be Indian, to live white, to be two persons at the same time was too much to ask of him. He wanted to hide far away. But from the cave, he could still see the fires and the shadowed figures that leaped and shouted in the ecstasies of the white man's religion. He shut his eyes. The sound of the hymns pierced him, hurt him. He covered his ears with his small thick hands. He backed away from the light and noise. He kept a bottle of whiskey deep inside the cave. There the old gods fought the white man's god, there Orpheus forsook the struggle and carefully unscrewed the top and let the white fire slide down his throat. Each slow drink pushed the battle further away and soon the voices were silent. Orpheus crawled deep into the keyhole where he slept secure.

Voices came again, awful voices full of hate and terror. But they went away when he covered his head with his arms and moved deeper within the earth.

When Orpheus awoke, he crawled toward the whiskey bottle, found it nearly empty, but the cave was full of a bloody smell, and rags were strewn about. Outside the late summer rain curtained the entrance. He walked into the wetness to cool his burning head and body. He washed himself in the absolution of whichever god had provided. The rain was good, healing as he turned his wide red face up into it. When he finally moved down the path, fear greater than his earlier fear of the preacher closed its icy fingers around his heart.

Dead children. Dead white children lay under the out-cropping below.

Pulling his knife, Orpheus wailed to the old gods for the children, for himself. He began to cut his flesh, his forearms, chest, legs, fast frantic cuts with a relieving pain.

Then he was tired, and he went back inside the cave. He jammed his knife into the stone wall till the blade snapped. He crawled back into the keyhole, carrying the bottle and the broken knife. Hunched in the blackness, drawing on the bottle, he threw the knife and listened to it bounce on the stones. The voices came again. He sat listening. Fear ran through him as he realized they were real and coming near. He kicked the rocks with his foot. The noise deafened him as he crawled through the hole toward the hall. Then Orpheus McKee started to run toward the light, toward the thicket.

Shank lay quietly beside Susan, listening to the soft sweet sound of her breathing. He did not sleep, but looked at the ceiling, at the play of moonlight on the papered walls. His town and his contentment were dying. For the first time in his adult life, Shank was angry, not irritable or cross, but angry to his center. He tried to push his thoughts into calm and turned restlessly. Finally he got up, pulled on his trousers and went downstairs.

He sat in the rocker by the window and tried to center down, to focus his mind on listening for the still small voice. And the voice was the confusion that ran through his mind. Anger crowded in, pushed, intruded. People could not so easily throw away who they were, what they had built together. And then he remembered the faces in the closed circle, in Bryan's store. And he knew they could, perhaps they already had.

He must not let such destruction of his town happen. He would not. He would find Orpheus McKee and bring him in. Jud Lewis and his poison would go away. But, Josh thought, they would not go. There would be the trial, long and brutal, coating Shiloh again with hate and mistrust.

If Orpheus were dead, that would be an end—the murderer found and dead. Shiloh would go peacefully on. The stores would prosper. The corn, fat cattle and apples would grow. The children would go back to school. The sound of singing would roll across First Day morning. If Orpheus were dead.

Shank would go alone, and track Orpheus as he had tracked the marauding bear when he was sixteen. It had been after the War's end when times were at their worst in the border country. Nobody had any money and everything had to be bought. The armies, North and South, and the guerillas had burned or carried off everything of value and butchered every chicken, cow and pig. What crops had been put out fared poorly.

There was hunger and death in most homes that winter. Men and women weakened by the War, and the work gave in to disease and despair. But worse than the disease of the body was the disease of the soul—the distrust of neighbor for neighbor. The color of a man's pants made him a target for other men. Suspicion of past betrayals and retribution kept men close to home and kin, careful of their words in company. The suspicions and mistrust kept the people from working together against their common enemies.

Shank sometimes helped with his father's school, rebuilding it after it was burned, but few children came. There was no money for school, and no trust for the man who ran it. As much as the Yank hated the Reb, they both hated the Quaker schoolteacher. Maybe they hated him for not fighting or maybe for being above the fight, like he was too smart or too good. Or maybe they hated him because he managed a small prosperity in the midst of their poverty. They spat tobacco through stained teeth as the elder Shank passed by. Young Joshua grew hard and bitter inside at what he saw and what he felt of the hatred.

The boys cast him out from their company, calling him coward because of his belief that war settled nothing. Quatie Rose's father ran Shank and LeFevre away from her after Pea Ridge. Carter Rose called him a traitor and LeFevre a white-trash pup. Gradually LeFevre and Shank went their separate ways. Le-

Fevre's ma died, and he had to get food enough just to live. He didn't have much time to be a boy then, no time for boys' battles. Shank never blamed LeFevre for keeping clear. He knew he had his own troubles. Finally LeFevre wandered off to Silam and began to clerk and read law with Judge Terry. Judge Terry kind of adopted him, too, taking him for the son he had lost at Gettysburg with Hood's cavalry.

Shank grew taller, past six foot, and lean and hard from working long days on the farm and from the endless nights he followed his hounds across the hills. He knew the border country better than any man. Sometimes covering twenty-five miles in a night, his hunting brought good pelts for trading or money. In the hills Shank passed from childhood, from self-pity and bitterness, as he found a man's confidence in his courage and skills.

He didn't avoid Shiloh any longer. Shank found he could look a man in the eye and make him think before he said coward. Shank dropped the plain language he used with his Quaker family because it called attention to him, because instead of making men equals as it had once intended, it made him seem superior in piety.

In the winter of '68 the men of Shiloh took every coin from their pockets to buy five scrawny Texas beeves. By dividing the slaughtered herd, they hoped it would last till spring. The day the cowboy drove the steers into Shiloh was Christmas Eve. Snow was falling softly covering the scarred, burned out buildings. Pettigrew Willis rang the Shiloh bells. Threadbare coats did not keep the cold out, but the people of Shiloh went in jubilation through the winter twilight to admire the penned up cattle. Shank watched from Bryan's store, then silently walked home past the empty school listening to the merry bells.

"Take this cake to Clary, Joshua," Shank's mother said in the morning. "It is small Christmas for good friends, but it is all we can spare."

Shank held the last biscuit and honey in his mouth as he put on his skin coat. He walked swiftly to Shiloh, carrying the cake in one hand, his rifle in the other.

The new snow meant easy tracking. He might scare up a red-fox for a real Christmas present or a turkey for dinner.

Shank saw the Shiloh men gathered silently around the cattle pen. He eased into the group with Tom Bryan. The cattle were all dead; they had been ripped to shreds, maliciously torn, squandered and eaten.

"My god," said Tom. "We'll not be able to save much. Damn bear. Damn, damn bear."

Suddenly Shank was mad, mad at the bear, mad at the men who stood defeated before the pen. He shoved the cake into Bryan's belly. "I'll need some shells, Tom," he said.

Bryan looked at the tough young face, trying to place it and the words. "Josh, you can't go after that bear. It's a giant. It's a killer, son. Besides, there's nothing to gain. The cattle are dead and the money's all gone."

"It's to be done, Tom, or we're all beat. I'll get the shells from Clary. Tell Pa where I went, please," Shank said. Bryan watched him head off toward the store.

Shank followed the bear for five days, five freezing days and colder nights when he slept sitting, huddled in caves before a hatful of fire. A bear doesn't get to be so big or so mean by being stupid. It knew a man tracked him, but underestimated its enemy—a Quaker boy with a single shot rifle. On the fifth day, as Shank moved through a dense thicket, the bear raised up to its full height pawing the air. Shank did not run. He backed away carefully, put the gun to his shoulder, sighted and fired, hitting the bear squarely between the eyes. It swayed then staggered, still standing, toward Shank. Shank backed away, stepped behind a tree, and began to reload the rifle, looking back at the bear. "Fall, damn your wanton soul," he said, and raised the gun again and walked toward the bear. It straightened suddenly and fell. Shank waited, then approached carefully and finished the animal off. He skinned it, cut up the carcass.

Finally Shank made a sled and dragged the bear back to Shiloh. He divided the small amount of meat

at Bryan's store among the cattle owners. If the meat
pots were thin that winter, they were nevertheless satisfied with a certain knowledge that no intruder could
come to Shiloh without paying the price. After that no
man called Shank coward; no man held the words in
his thoughts. When spring came there was less suspicion in Shiloh, and the town began to get well.

Rocking softly now in his sitting room, Shank was
mesmerized by the vision of taking his gun, tracking
McKee and shooting him in some wilderness grove. He
saw it clearly. McKee's heart resting atop Shank's
gunsights as he eased the hammer back, lay his thumb
alongside and, holding his breath, squeezed the trigger.
Orpheus falling slowly, turning with the impact of the
bullet, searching the woods for the assassin. His black
eyes burning into the woods and finding Shank.

"I am no animal," his dying lips said. "I am a
man."

Shank blinked away the vision. He had settled. His
inner voice had spoken. McKee was, after all, a man.
Unless Shank could deny that, to kill him like a beast
would destroy the hunter and his world, as well as the
prey. The town was more than shops, farms, church
and school. It was men living by laws, ordering their
lives for themselves but also in relation to others to
their good. If the relation was broken, the shops,
farms, church and school were empty forms, meaning-
less conveniences to partake or discard at will. The
sacrifice of McKee would not save the town; it would
destroy it. He must be found and brought back alive.
The matter had to be clearly settled without doubts or
maybes.

The young Shank would have known it, seen it with
the clear eyes of youth. LeFevre knew it had to be
solved if Shiloh was to survive. He knew it on the
porch at Bryan's Store when he sent Shank after the
dog posse. It was the first time in seven years LeFevre
had clung to justice again. LeFevre had been afraid of
bright blinding dreams like justice since he lost Quatie
Rose to the law, more afraid because she put her life
down for some honor within her. He had fought to

save her from the beautiful law he loved. She had
refused his skill, bypassing man's accumulated statutes
and precedents for truth, taking the crazy hard Cherokee way of affirming right by confirming her guilt.

That summer Quatie had shot and killed William
Bell, wounded his wife India, and his grown son, Emmet, as they came out of the theatre in Silam. No one
knew why. Quatie Rose never said. At the trial she
stood quietly in the witness box and never said more
than that she did the deed. She had been shot, too.
And LeFevre found witnesses who saw Bell fire first.
But he couldn't get around the fact that Quatie had
taken a gun to town intending to deal with Bell. The
jury wanted to see Will LeFevre win. But in the end,
his victory sent Quatie to the Detroit Prison for Wom-
en for seven years and LeFevre on a seven year drunk.

Justice was a double edged sword, and the bright
blinding dream called civilization carried a dear price
for LeFevre and Quatie. But where was it written that
it would be otherwise? Where did a man gracefully
step down from his life's dreams and say this is enough
for me, you boys go on without me? A man couldn't
get off. He could only go on or be lost. Life was the
painful, arduous and fearful task of working out a
relation with things bigger than a man, with God,
maybe. There was just no place where a man could sit
back. Shank could no longer be content with his well-
ordered world. He'd lost himself somewhere, forgotten
what his Pa used to say that the one thing worse than
failing to practice what we preach is watering down
our preaching to match our practice. The dreams were
out there somewhere still waiting, but different from a
boy's dreams. They were stronger and tougher and
more than a boy could handle. It took a man to face
the reality of a dream, to win it with his sweat and
blood and failure—and his love.

The unlocked front door swung open. Shank rose
from the rocker as Quatie Rose stepped out of the
moonlight and into the room.

"George says Indians can't come to Shiloh after

sunset," she said. "He says the trash from Silam ran off Frank Starr and Ross Walker. He says you stood up for us."

"I didn't do much good. Adeyaheh poisons the Cherokee and Herb Latta and Jud Lewis the whites."

"You don't believe in witches?" Quatie's tone was full of a mild derision of the idea. "Witches that help killers hide."

"I believe that evil grows in men who cultivate it."

"You don't believe a witch killed the children?"

"I believe a man killed them."

"Then you and I are the only white or Cherokee who do. The Adeyaheh controls the Indians again because only he can charm the witch. Even Starr and Walker's voices are silent now. It is as he would have it, like the old days when Cherokees feared and hated the whites instead of each other."

Shank struck a match and lit the table lamp bringing a faint light to the room. Quatie's black cape completely wrapped her small body. She was more beautiful than he remembered. The tragedy of the past years had refined her features, changing her from a willful girl into a strong woman. Hers was beauty that time would little alter, for it came from a presence within her. She wore it as she wore the cloak, holding it upright with something inside. As Josh closed the door he saw three dogs sitting obediently on the porch. George's son sat on the steps.

"You found the bodies and tolled the bells, didn't you, Quatie?"

"Yes. Little George gave me their names. We were looking for lambs lost in the storm."

"Did you see Orpheus?"

"We saw no one except the dead."

"When you found them were they laid out?"

"No, they were thrown on the ground like Ross Walker's child. Thrown away. We left her for the law, but moved the others into the overhang. I think he killed her first or maybe last. He separated her body from theirs although he treated them the same. We saw a shadow going across Sleepy Creek. For a while there was a heel mark in the sand, but the rain took it."

"Was the print going toward camp?" Quatie nodded. "Does Orpheus wear boots or moccasins?"

"Boots, I suppose, like any man who lives in these rocky hills."

"I must find Orpheus and bring him in for trial before this town is torn apart."

Quatie turned the heavy glass paperweight on Shank's desk. She considered the bright flowers immortalized in glass as she asked, "How did the dogs act yesterday on the trail?"

"They lost the scent. One seemed overcome by the heat. One was scared and hid from us. He acted like he was seeing things."

"I think someone who knows potions mixed blood with cocaine and drugged the animals."

"Cocaine?"

"One can easily buy the drug in Fort Smith behind the courthouse on Coke Hill. It can be taken through the nose. The dogs were on a scent."

"But who would know?" The words faded from Shank's mouth as the realization of who would know came. "The Adeyaheh?"

"He knows where Orpheus is," Quatie said quietly.

Chapter Six

Shank lay on his belly in the humus of years of undisturbed leaves. Rocks and little bushes grew on the cliff above the Adeyaheh's cabin, but no grass. Quatie was silent, intent on the scene below. George's son was with them.

"You're sure this is his place?" Shank asked.

"This is where he lives. But Orpheus will not be inside. We must follow the Adeyaheh from here. He is a fox, that old one."

"Quatie, why are you doing this for us? After all that's happened to you, the trial, prison?"

She turned on her side and looked at Shank. "Is life any less mine than yours? Can it run me off with threats of more pain and make me a coward as well as an outcast? I have not left the earth, Joshua Shank. I will see this through. Look," she said as her gaze returned to the cabin. "He is coming out."

Shank and Quatie watched the Adeyaheh throw dirty water from a dish pan into the yard. He puttered around on the little porch, hanging up the pan on the wall and stretching the dish towel and rag over a wire. He checked herbs growing in rusty cans on the porch and went back inside. In a while he re-emerged carrying a tow sack.

"That's medicine roots for Bryan's store," Shank said. "I've seen him bring them in before. He's going to town. Let's go."

"Follow him, Shank. He may turn off. I'll wait here in case he circles back. If he comes, I'll send Little George to find you."

Shank glanced at the tall thin black youngster.

"You find me quick, George," he said and walked off after the conjurer.

Shank followed the old man from the wooded ridge and back a short way. The Adeyaheh held straight to

the path for a mile then paused, looked around him
and turned up the ridge opposite Shank. Watching him
climb, Shank waited for him to take a path that he
could follow without being seen himself. The Indian
finally topped the ridge. Shank guessed he would lie
there until he was sure no one followed. The Indian
held the advantage. He could stay on the ridge and
discover his pursuer or he could leave while the tracker
waited.

Shank looked about him. Far down the valley, the
distance between the ridges was smaller, obscured from
the other ridge by a limestone outcropping. To move at
all he would have to get there and try to find the old
creator of spells before he got away.

It took Shank a half hour to cross the valley and
climb the limestone ridge. By slow steady movement
among the trees and boulders he came within sight of
the spot where he had last seen the Adeyaheh. He
watched the woods for a long time. The old one was
gone. Shank moved slowly from his cover into the trail.
He looked for a track, turned up rocks, a broken stalk,
but the prey had led him to and escaped across a sheet
of pure stone.

Shank studied the evil mountain beyond him. The
Indians said its myriad caves were homes for evil
spirits, holes left when they were driven off by the
gods, when the corruption was cleansed. The settlers
took the legend and called the place Devil's Legion
from their Bible. "My name is Legion; for we are
many," said the Gerasene demoniac as Jesus cast his
evil spirits into a herd of swine. And so the cave-
corrupted mountain became Devil's Legion, purified,
yet tainted by the memory of many evils.

Pocket caves penetrated the mountain's surface.
Any of them could hide a man, lead into the earth or
through it to another opening. Shank did not like the
caves. The dark stillness of them made him feel buried
alive. He had never sought them for recreation, not
even as a boy. When he entered one it was usually for a
purpose.

He sat down. Yesterday the dogs had been stopped
fifty yards below the caves. The men had gone on

awhile then turned back in the face of night and the sheer number of caves. Josh thought. Only three of the caves were deep. One snaked into the earth, opening into spacious rooms and ending in an underground stream. The other two were dead ends as far as he knew, but nonetheless complex enough to hide a man within their caverns. The cave with the stream was near where the dogs had stopped.

Shank cut across country, forsaking the possibility of finding the Adeyaheh's trail. He was betting the old man had gone straight to the river cave. He could easily hide a man there. If his enemies discovered him, the fugitive could take the back door out by swimming underwater. The stream was deep. From there a man could float away to the Arkansas and the Mississippi, completely leaving the hill country and the debt he owed.

When Shank reached the entrance of the river cave, he checked for signs. He quickly found a well-shaped moccasin track in the loose dirt. Looking about in the entrance, he found the Indian's stash of pine knots. Shank pulled a sulphur match from his pocket and lit the torch. He headed into the depths of the cave. He did not plan to surprise his prey, only to reach him with the greatest speed possible. Going over the mountain to the other entrance would take another two hours.

He wished LeFevre had not broken his ankle, that Whiting was not keeping tabs on Jud Lewis. Together they could have rigged it so no one escaped the cave. But Josh had to go alone. He knew Orpheus and the Adeyaheh would not be afraid of him and run. He carried no weapons. He hoped Orpheus would listen to him, give himself up and return with him to Shiloh. Shank was sure that he and Whiting and LeFevre along with Tom Bryan and a few others could protect Orpheus from a lynch mob until he could be transferred and tried.

The cave was cold. The walls were wet and slick. Shank walked swiftly through the dark halls. In the inner chambers, he paused and held the torch high as he turned to survey the rooms. The walls and ceilings sparkled as the light touched their crystal surfaces. The sight had made Shank catch his breath as a boy. It still did. He went on from chamber to chamber until he stood in the hall above the river room. He listened, but heard only the rushing water. When he emerged onto the rocks above the chamber floor he found the room empty. He held his torch toward the walls. The water glowed faintly as it carried the only other light into the blackness.

Shank slipped off the rocks onto the floor. Holding the torch high again, he looked for any sign of habitation. He saw the fire hole close to the stream. Everyone used it, picking up sticks and driftwood and building a fire to cook fish or heat coffee or just to sit beside. Shank touched the center of the hole. The ashes were cold. He ran his hand along the rock sides of the pit searching for any warmth. It was cold. No one had used it lately. Orpheus had not been here. The Adeyaheh had tricked Shank. Planting the footprint and pine knot torches had put Shank off the trail and led him into the wrong cave. Shank shrugged and dropped the torch into the fire hole.

"One for you, old man," he said.

It was afternoon before Shank returned to Shiloh. At Bryan's store he learned the Adeyaheh had sold his forest herbs and bought coffee and flour with the small amount of money. The sheriff and his posse were checking a sighting at the Baker place. Shank went home to change his boots and eat. He needed to think.

Susan's wash flapped gently in the summer breeze. She left her basket to come to Josh.

"Is this wash day?" he asked.

"No," she said, looking at her apron front.

"Thee works hardest when thee is troubled." Josh looked at Susan's soft, serene face and touched the smooth pinkness of her cheek.

He had left so abruptly last night with Quatie Rose that he had barely said more to Susan than he was going. It was not a thoughtful thing he had done, but it had been the action to take in the circumstances.

Standing now in his yard, he knew he owed his wife an explanation.

"Let's sit in the shade," he said, putting his arm comfortably around Susan's slender waist. "Where's Noah?"

"He's fishing on Sleepy Creek with Joe Whiting."

They sat in the speckled shade near the stone spring house. The air was still and fresh. Shank stretched out his long legs and reached into his pocket for a handkerchief. He removed his broad brimmed hat and began to wipe sweat from the brow band.

"I used to fish a lot when I was Noah's age. Same place I bet, just below Pin Oak. My friends were Will LeFevre and Quatie Rose. Quatie didn't like fishing much, but she liked Will and had to protect him from snakes. Will's always been scared of snakes. He'd freeze stone still, and she'd come with a couple of sticks. She'd get the snake to strike one and bash his head in with the other. Then she'd go back to her book or handwork.

"I wish you could have known Quatie then. She was small and fragile and brave, braver than us boys sometimes.

"Once Tad and Taugh Davis caught Will and me and took our string of fish. They'd seen us buy a bag of candy at Bryant's and wanted it too. We had it hidden and wouldn't tell where it was. So they were holding us under in the creek till we did. Quatie came down from the house about then.

"'Release them instantly!' she commanded. The Davis twins looked up surprised and let up on us a bit.

"'Aw shoot, she's jest a little girl,' Taugh said. 'She ain't important.'

"'I'm important to me,' Quatie said and fire danced in her eyes. She came down the hill like the Furies, waving a stick, throwing rocks and setting the dogs on the Davis boys. That was just what Will and I needed. We took them by storm. We weren't smaller anymore. We were three against two. We were fiercer. Between us we sent them home without the candy or the fish and with a few bruises. They never came back again.

"Quatie was with us, but she was alone, too. Alone because she wasn't a boy, and wasn't allowed to do some things, and she didn't know any girls. She only had me and Will and a bunch of animals for friends and her brothers at home. Of course, they were a lot older than she was so they ignored her or spoiled her by turns.

"Her father wasn't home much. He had business dealings in Arkansas, especially after the secession talk started. Quatie's mother died when she was seven. So she'd stay with Will and me till she'd had enough human company, and she'd go home. Nobody'd be there but the Negroes, but she'd go. Would never come to my house or Will's for dinner. Carter Rose didn't allow her to associate much. From the few things I saw, she'd rather accept his law than put her friends in danger of his wrath.

"I still see her going up that long hill toward Pin Oak, a little girl in a polka dot dress all alone except for the critters that followed her everywhere."

"But Josh, that little girl in a polka dot dress grew up to kill a man and shoot his wife and son," Susan said. "And that is not gossip, Josh. She went to prison."

Josh looked straight into Susan's eyes. "Quatie never denied her guilt. But there was more to it than people have told you. After her brothers were killed in the War, Carter Rose went kind of mad with grief and set out to make Quatie take their places. For years he'd ignored her, and suddenly she had to be made into his heir. If life was tough before, it became a lot tougher. Carter ran a hard school at Pin Oak. Finally, he sent her away to study and then to his relatives in England to complete the education.

"She was gone a long time, ten years maybe. I saw her twice when she came back, once at Carter's funeral, once in the courtroom. LeFevre tried to defend her, but she kept saying she shot Bell. I guess that was the Indian in her. If a witness hadn't seen Bell reach for his gun first, she might have hung. She'd never have asked for mercy, never have explained anything. Nobody ever knew why they quarreled. There was so much bad feeling here after the war. Folks thought maybe it was over land in Arkansas or over her father and brothers' stand in the war. I truly don't know, Susan."

"But she killed the man, Josh. She killed." Susan's soft brow was creased with an unaccustomed frown.

"That's the fact. And for some folks that's enough. But it may not be the truth. Susan, Quatie would not have killed Bell lightly, not over land or an insult to her family. Whatever made her kill was too terrible for her to live with or to talk about in court. There's still a story to be told."

"And Josh, you going off with her in the middle of the night. She must hold her reputation very lightly." Susan finally came to her own problem with Quatie Rose.

Josh sat back, a little shocked by Susan's words. "Thee is jealous of me and Quatie? Why, Susan. Quatie's not like that. She isn't like other women. Her thoughts don't come from the same places or experiences. She was raised to be a man, to think like a man, and because she's a woman that sets the local women's teeth on edge. They don't know her or understand her, but they judge her by their small standards of the way a woman should act. Quatie doesn't want me or any of their husbands. She's always loved Will, and someday they'll get straightened out. She'd no more steal affections than she'd rob your money. Why, Susan, Quatie's been all over the world. She's read books people here never heard of. She's talked to men who will shape the thoughts of generations. Do you seriously think she has no more character than to seduce wayward husbands or lure backwoods bachelors? My god, Susan."

Shank stood up. He was uncomfortable and a little irritated that his Susan would listen to gossip and apply it to him.

"I won't tell thee what to think, Susan. I never have. I only tell thee what I know. I know Quatie is a lady with breeding and courage and honor. Too much honor to choose the low road. And right now she's the only person in Shiloh who's thinking about justice instead of revenge or self-interest. She's the only help I've got besides you and Will, and I feel lucky she's our friend."

Quatie Rose sent Little George to Pin Oak for food and a book. She passed the day pleasantly enough, reading and watching. At dusk, she put the book aside and lay down to watch for the old Indian's return.

The Adeyaheh came slowly down the trail he had left that morning. He still carried the sack, but leaned more heavily on his staff. Quatie watched the light come on in the cabin, smelled the hominy and fat back from his supper. The moon was low behind the hills to the east, and the valley was black except for the lamp in the cabin. Quatie fidgeted. He would go out again. She was sure.

Shank had sent word of his own fruitless pursuit. The old man had misled whoever might follow—that meant he knew where Orpheus was. His late morning visit to the store meant he had not stopped except to misguide his follower. He had saved his visit for the cover of darkness and spent the afternoon visiting with Orpheus' sister. By now he knew Shank was the tracker. But she doubted he knew about her.

"Come on, George," Quatie said. "We've got to get closer to see him leave."

She and the black youth made their way down the timbered slope toward the cabin. They found a place viewing the back door.

"See if you can find a place where you can see the front," she told George. "If he comes out whistle a signal."

Quatie watched George move easily among the trees and disappear, then turned to watch the door. The light in the cabin went out, and the muscles in Quatie's body tightened. He was getting ready, waiting for them to think he was asleep. A quarter hour passed, and she heard George's signal. She walked quickly in the direction he had gone.

"Over here, Miss Quatie," George whispered. "He went into the creek and walked up that way."

Quatie looked in the direction Little George pointed. "Good," she said. "Get Josh Shank, tell him what you saw and bring him back."

"Yes, ma'am," George said and slipped into the night.

Quatie crossed the cabin yard and walked slowly into the stream. It was only ankle deep, but icy cold. She gasped and shivered with the chill, but set her shoulders for the walk feeling still Indian enough to endure. The banks were too steep and narrow to walk along. She had to take the cold and treacherous waterway as the Adeyaheh had done. If she could sight him or hear him without being discovered herself, she could use him as a guide through the stream.

Quatie walked carefully over the rocky bottom trying not to stumble, bracing herself with the shepherd's staff she carried, testing for deep holes in the stream bed. Her skirt's hem was soaked and cumbersome. Women's clothes were an impedance. Gradually the stream deepened until she was wading in thigh-deep water. Pushing the water, pulling the skirts made her feel suspended, exerting total energy for minimum movement. But she had spotted the old man ahead and held persistently to the trail. The moon was higher and she could see him clearly through the trees. He held his course through the middle of the stream, but Quatie tried to hold to the tree-protected banks. She moved carefully, tense with the fear of losing the old man or of being caught.

The Adeyaheh had never been her friend. She had defied him by bringing white medicine to the sick. She had refused to bow to his superstitions. She had encouraged the women to raise hens and sheep, to grow cotton, to spin and weave the wool and fibre to sell and to clothe their families. Now that she was back, the war between them had started again.

Easing along the bank in the cold water, she jumped suddenly as a bullfrog leaped into the safety of the water. She held her hand to her chest as she caught the breath which had leaped from her body like the frog. Again she moved on, keeping the old man in view through the trees. Memories of snakes along the water banks put fear into her mind.

The moon rose higher. By this time George might have found Shank, Quatie thought. Before leaving the trees that hid her, she watched the Adeyaheh round a small bend. As she stepped out, a heavy branch snapped into her face, cutting it below the high cheek bone, sending her helplessly back against the rocky banks. Then a shadow was upon her, hitting her about the head with a smooth river stone, pounding her with rock and fist until she lay unconscious.

Chapter Seven

"Did you hear something?" Shank asked Little George.

"Yes, sir, sounded like a moan."

Shank stood listening as his eyes searched the bank. A movement, the sound of rocks shifting, led him to Quatie. He bent and looked at her. Her face and scalp were covered with blood. He pushed the matted hair from her eyes. She opened them and her hand caught his shirt.

"Two. There are two," she whispered.

Shank lifted her into his arms, wrestling with the weight of the wet skirts.

"This way, Mr. Shank," said young George. "We can cut across here and take her to Pin Oak."

"Yes. I know the way. You go for Doctor Clark," Shank said, struggling up the rocky bank. His long legs carried him swiftly through the night.

Shank kicked the double walnut doors at Pin Oak with his muddy boot. Quatie, unconscious again, lay limp and lifeless in his arms. Inside he heard the dogs.

Unlike most civilized folk, Quatie allowed dogs in her house. She kept a special dog room in the basement where they were washed more often than some of her neighbors and ate better food from cleaner bowls. The mixed-breed shepherds were her associates in the sheep raising business, her wards in God's eyes, and her pleasure. When she was away in prison, George and his wife Des had kept Quatie's world, including the kennels, intact.

Inside Josh heard Des' deep voice. "Hush. Hush, dog. I'm comin'." She opened the door and gasped at the tall Quaker holding Quatie in his arms. "Sakes, Mr. Joshua. Bring her up here. Shoo, dog," she said, brushing past the old dog now wagging its tail.

Des climbed the spiral staircase that wrapped
through the entrance hall to the family quarters upstairs. Josh followed, strongly aware of his muddy
boots and Quatie's dripping skirts on the flowered
carpets. He held Quatie as Des turned back the bed
covers. He lay the woman gently on the freshly ironed
sheets.

"What happened to her?" Des asked as she looked
at her mistress' head. "Little George say she was
watchin' that ol' spell-maker. That old witcher do
this?"

"I don't know. We found her like this in the creek."

"Mr. Joshua, you get some water and towels over
there while I gets Miss Quatie out of these wet
clothes."

Shank walked toward the chest Des had indicated.
A china pitcher and bowls painted with roses sat on
the pale pink marble top. Seeing no towels, he opened
the doors of the cabinet. The inside was packed with
fine towels, monogrammed with a large intertwined
"QR." The cabinet smelled of roses and herbs.

"Bandages and dressings are in the little box in the
bottom of the chifferobe," Des called over her shoulder.

The Abusson carpet was thick and lush under
Shank's boots as he moved to the huge chest. He saw
his disheveled appearance in its mirrored front. He
removed his wide brimmed hat and laid it on the pink
velvet settee. Inside the chest the same scent of roses
and herbs reached him. Quatie's dresses hung neatly
across the interior. He stooped to search the cabinet's
floor for the box of bandages and medicine. He had to
push the dresses aside to see. On the floor were Quatie's slippers and a large open box that contained a
wooden gun LeFevre had made at ten and carved his
initials into. Shank paused. Quatie had saved frag-
ments of their childhood. He looked deeper, pushing
aside the toys, remembering. A shooter made from a
tree fork, twine and a strip of rubber belonged to Josh.
A tobacco bag held his magic marbles. There was a
broken rusty pocket knife that LeFevre had found. A
rag doll soiled and torn was in the box, too.

"You still lookin'?" Des was at his side. Her eyes followed his gaze. "She keeps those special. Dolls and stuff like that goes in the playroom. But you boys and Millie's things she keeps here. They been there since the day Mister Carter run you boys off from Quatie. Won't let me throw 'em out. Gets fussy if I move 'em."

Des found the bandage box and returned to the bed where Quatie lay in a high necked white gown. Shank carried the water pitcher and towels, taking care not to slosh water on the carpet. Quatie looked small and very pale as Des began to wash the head wounds.

"That cut's gonna leave a scar," Des said.

Shank walked to the windows that opened on a small balcony. Swiss lace curtains hung over the sparkling glass. He turned the brass handle and stepped out onto the iron balcony. It was small and strong and offered a perfect view of the driveway and the coming doctor.

Quatie's room ran the length of the house with window balconies on the front and a wide wrought iron veranda on the back. It was a foreign architecture to the hill country, more suitable to Charleston or New Orleans or Europe. But it had suited Quatie's father, and he had built it of brick, iron and fine wood long before she was born. He had come through the Trail of Tears with the other mixed Cherokees, but his household had ridden in carriages and on fine horses. Their slaves had made the trip as comfortable as possible for the Roses. Their suffering had been minimal because their money had been secure in foreign banks.

Carter Rose's grandfather was an Englishman accustomed to control, and hungry for the wealth that had gone to his elder brother. He had made his fortune in the New World and secured it for his mixed blood progeny in land, money, education and drive. Georgia and the United States had seized the rich plantation lands, but Carter Rose prospered on the money, education and inherited drive of his grandfather.

Josh remembered the old aristocrat. He had been meticulous in his dress and household. Quatie had inherited that compulsion for order. She had also inherited the sense of justice that, when outraged, led to violent temper. It had led her to kill William Bell and shoot his wife and son on the square at Silam.

Carter Rose had not known. He had died in the autumn of 1870, full of years. A tormented man, he had seen his two sons die at Pea Ridge. When Watie's Indians had retreated, they had stayed. They had died together, leaving Carter Rose with a young daughter to build his hopes on. He drove her, compelled her to learn every detail of running Pin Oak. He sent her to eastern schools, and to Europe. When she returned, she was a seasoned observer of the human scene, accustomed to wealth and power, disciplined to take her place. But she returned alone with the tension and hate of the years within her.

The rattle of wheels recalled Josh's thoughts to the driveway. He saw Doctor Clark alight from the carriage. Young George handed him his bag and snapped the horse's lead to the tying weight. Shank started to go downstairs, but turned back to see a pair of crutches thrown from the buggy and LeFevre appear, cast first. Shank smiled. LeFevre loved Quatie. When she was helpless, when she could not send him away, he came.

"God bless Will LeFevre," Shank thought and went to the stairs.

Doc Clark made his way quickly up to Quatie. Shank sat down to wait for LeFevre, who struggled with the stairs on his crutches.

"Goddamn, sonofabitch to hell," Shank heard LeFevre swear. "LeFevre you're a stupid sonofabitch for breakin' your own damn leg."

"Want some help?" Josh asked.

"Hell, no, I'm used to it," LeFevre said, getting the system for climbing stairs. "How bad is it?" he asked, at last turning and dropping to the wide stair by Shank.

"I think she'll be fine, but somebody tried to bash her head in."

"That damned old Indian?"

"Don't think so. She said there were two. Must have been she was following him and somebody else was waiting."

"That old varmint," LeFevre muttered. "Why was she following him?"

"She thinks he's hiding Orpheus McKee somewhere."

"Then Orpheus must have done it. That no good . . ."

"She'll be good as new in a few days, men," Doctor Clark announced as he started down the stairs. "Shank, she wants to talk to you."

"Thanks, Doc."

"I knew that damned hard head of hers would come in handy some day," said LeFevre, hobbling behind Shank.

Quatie was pale even against the embroidery and lace pillowcase. Shank saw a row of stitches along her hairline and on her cheek, but most of her injuries were bruises, purple-red and angry on the soft skin. Her hand caught his sleeve and she pulled him closer. When she spoke her voice was soft and tired but clear and precise.

"Josh, there's somebody else. Somebody we hadn't figured on. Whoever caught me wasn't Orpheus or the Adeyaheh. He had short hair. He was lean and strong. Not too tall. I think I scratched his neck and chest, and tore his shirt. But it was fast and very dark under the trees. Josh, I think he's white."

Quatie's gaze went past Shank to LeFevre. She smiled, then caught herself and frowned weakly.

"LeFevre. I haven't the strength to run you off now."

LeFevre hopped forward easing the crutch to the floor, and caught Quatie's hand. "That's right, Quatie. You can't run me off again." His voice was different, as it always was with Quatie. She had closed her eyes, but still gripped his hand. "I'll stay with her, Josh. Do what you got to do."

Shank pushed open the door to the Adeyaheh's shack. The sparsely furnished room was empty. The bed was still made. The fireplace was cold and empty. Shank stepped through the doorway and walked through the house to the back. The old man's hungry chickens ran eagerly to the door as Shank opened it and looked out. The old conjurer had not come back last night. That was plain to Shank. He walked around the cabin and remounted his horse. She threw her head a few times against the reins, eager and fresh with the morning. Her rider sat looking about, then nudged her side and guided her into Sleepy Creek.

The mare splashed through the cold shallow water, her hoofs making a sweet hollow sound against the rocks. In a little while, Shank spotted the place where he had found Quatie. He dismounted and searched the bank in the early morning light. The bank was dug up. Bushes were crushed and broken. He found a stone with blood and hair still stuck to it. He threw it into the creek and watched it settle among the spreading ripples. The water was clear and something white fluttered with the motion of the descending rock. Shank bent closer then stuck his hand into the current. He retrieved a piece of fabric clinging to a broken branch. Sitting back on his boots, he examined the dripping fragment. He dragged it between his fingers squeezing the water out, then held it up to the sun. It was silk, pure white silk. Had Quatie worn a silk petticoat? He tucked the cloth in his shirt pocket. Who besides Quatie wore silk in Shiloh?

Quatie lay listening to the sound of LeFevre's breathing from the settee. It was a quiet contented sound with bubbles at the end that she remembered from childhood. She saw Des dozing in the rocker. Then she closed her eyes against the pain in her head that made the room revolve and the mattress float on unknown seas. Her hand searched the night table for tablets and the half-full water glass. She pressed the pills into her mouth and drank the water to push them down. She settled back to wait for the pain to wash away.

Shank rode downstream, letting the horse pick its way among the stones. He rounded a slow bend and

looked up into the trees. He looked hard again, almost
sensing the presence of the tiny shack encompassed by
the eastern light. He turned the mare toward the bank
and encouraged her up the steep wall. In the woods he
dismounted and pushed open the weathered door of
the hut. The place smelled of fires and charms and
blood. Bunches of herbs and grasses hung from the
ceiling. Josh stepped inside, letting his eyes become
accustomed to the dark closet-like room. He took a
step then stumbled hard and fell sideways. The
Adeyaheh lay on his back, arm outstretched, still holding the brown sack, his face and neck blown away by a
shotgun's blast.

Josh sighed and wiped his mouth with his hand,
letting the backs of his fingers rest against his lips. He
propped his elbow on his knee and studied the scene
before him. Someone had been living here. There was
food on the log table, coffee on the fire. The corner
contained an unmade bed roll. When Josh found a
letter to McKee's sister among the bed rags, he was
sure Orpheus had lived in the cabin. But why had he
killed the Adeyaheh, his mentor? Josh studied the
letter. It contained the standard Cherokee greeting to
Orpheus' sister, then went on:

> *Do not believe what you hear of me. I am trying
> not to. I do not remember this killing business. I
> was drunk, but I think I would remember this
> thing. The old one says I am under a witch's
> power, but he knows who the witch is and will
> break his spell when he comes.*
>
> *I give you all that is mine since I must soon
> go away from here. I would like Willard to have
> my new hat with the wide brim. I must . . .*

The letter was unfinished. Josh folded it and put it
into his shirt.

He wrapped the Adeyaheh in the bed rags and
carried him to the horse and led the horse back the
way he had come. In the last few days Josh had seen
carnage that reminded him of the battlefield at Prairie

Grove. He and his family had searched the charred blown-out acres for the living among the dead. It was stupid, and it made him sick and angry. He kicked a rock, sending it clattering across the stones. He wanted to kill the part of man that makes him kill, that stirs him up against another. He wanted to take all the wanton, senseless killers and destroy them, annihilate them so the rest could live in peace. He wanted to, just as he had on the battlefield as a boy. He clenched his fists until the short nails cut into his palms. He remembered his father, dusty, covered with the soldiers' blood, soot-stained cheeks streaked white by tears. He remembered the old Quaker shaking him, hugging him to his chest, taking his clenched fists in his broad hands.

"Do not be angry," he said to the boy. "There is anger enough. Do not look here for reason or right. We do not judge, Josh. We only see the needs of these men, men on both sides. Someone must help the suffering."

"I won't have war. I won't," the boy Shank had said. "I won't when I'm grown up. I won't let men find excuses to kill each other."

The elder Shank held the young hands and began to pry open the boy's tight hard fists. "Josh, open thy hands. The feeling in thee that makes thee want to strike a blow will draw anger from other men, and war will never end. Clear thyself first. Be a peacemaker, son—a fistkiller—stretching an open and innocent hand to thy fellow man. Then thee will remove the cause for violence."

"Quatie! Quatie, help me, Quatie," Millie said in Quatie's fevered dream. But Quatie ran, danced across the ground fog away from her sister's voice. "Here I am, Quatie," the voice said in front of her. "For God's sake, Quatie. For His sake."

"No," said Quatie. "No. Leave me be, nigger. Go away. Die. I hate you. Leave me alone."

"What you sayin', Miss Quatie?" Des asked, laying a gentle hand on Quatie's moist forehead. "Wake up

now. Wake up, baby." She shook Quatie, who opened
her eyes wild and lost. "Goodness, girl," Des continued, "We got to change your gown. You wet all over."

Quatie pushed her hand away and sat up. "Where's
LeFevre?"

"He went to get cleaned up and eat supper."

"Supper? What time is it?"

"It's nighttime, Miss Quatie."

Quatie was already stumbling out of bed toward the
door. Des ran after, catching Quatie as she flung open
the bedroom door and caught herself against the
frame.

"LeFevre! Will, come here!" she shouted.

"Miss Quatie, set down here," Des pulled her mistress onto the chair by the door and wrapped her shawl
about her. "That gown ain't decent."

"Get Will, Des. It's important," Quatie said.

Des ran toward the stairs sensing the strangeness in
Quatie, the old wildness. She started down yelling for
LeFevre, but he was already struggling with the bot-
tom steps.

"Hurry, Mr. William. Hurry!"

The crutches tangled LeFevre in his rush. "Hell," he
said and threw them aside. Holding the banister he
began to hop, then to put weight on the broken ankle.

"Get up there, Des. I'm coming."

Des was holding Quatie against the chair when Le-
Fevre made it to the door. He was white, covered with
sweat, and his straight brown hair was in his eyes.

"Get the bed ready," he said and stooped to lift
Quatie. "Why can't you stay put? Why can't you do
what you're supposed to?" He scolded Quatie as he
hobbled toward the bed. "She needs a dry gown,
Des."

"LeFevre, listen to me. I killed William Bell."

"I know, honey, but that's past. Now lie still."

"No, Will. Listen." Quatie shook. "I dreamed about
it just now. But it wasn't the gun or the killing this
time. It was my sister Millie. I saw her lying in the
mud, begging me to help, reaching out for me, and I
ran away. But I couldn't stay away. I came back, and I

took my sister's hand for the first time in my life. And we were both covered by mud and blood. Her blood ran over me and the ground."

"Quatie, rest. Please rest," LeFevre said.

"No. Not now." Quatie brushed the damp rag away. "Will, my sister was eleven years old. She was a little girl, Will. I never told, but Emmet Bell raped her. He raped a child. He threw her away in the woods. That's why I went to Silam to find him and shoot him. It's Emmet, Will. We've got to tell Josh."

She fell back at last, letting LeFevre wipe her forehead with the cloth.

LeFevre thought a minute, remembering Bell. He was a high-living mama's boy who loved the good life. He wore tailor-made clothes and soft calfskin boots and rode a fiery horse his Daddy bought him. He shunned the company of the Shiloh men his age, calling them ruffians. He was soft. He stayed in Silam or Little Rock mostly, near the power. Bell was obsessive, hating Indians, believing in plots against him. He always went armed and ready for any attack, unconvinced that no one wanted his life.

He was a grown man when LeFevre and Shank were kids fishing, idling in the spring sun. And then Will remembered, found his private memory of Emmet Bell. That spring, Bell trotted his fine gelding and hack down Shiloh Road near where the boys fished. A rabbit darted out, and the carriage wheel struck it, stunned it. The boys watched Bell jump from his seat and stomp the trapped rabbit's skull with his polished boot. LeFevre remembered Bell's face. He had enjoyed it.

He'd been shot in the leg at the theatre. But before the bandages were off, he'd climbed in a carriage at the cemetery and left Shiloh, supposedly for special treatment of the wound in New Orleans. His mother recovered enough to testify at the trial, but Emmet left only a brief deposition. India lived on in Shiloh while Quatie was in prison. In conversations at the general store she seemed to take a real pleasure in thinking of Quatie locked in the drab prison, trapped in a cage she could not escape while Emmet toured the continent and later joined U.S. Senator Drake and his Washington circle. Finally India moved away to be Emmet's hostess. He became a powerful man, influential with the Senator, if underhanded and self-seeking. Bell was one of the fellows who'd end up with all the money whichever side he had to take. Then a year ago while on a trip to Haiti, Bell had been lost overboard in a storm.

"Bell was lost at sea last year," LeFevre said. "He left here, and we heard he was drowned at sea."

"Did they find a body? No, they didn't find a body. That low life is back. Yes, he is, Will. I know he is." Quatie's eyes pleaded with LeFevre for belief.

"Good God," he said as the meaning penetrated his mind. "Emmet. He threw Jo Belle Walker away from the white children. Nobody hated Indians more than Emmet. Then you didn't start out to kill old man Bell in a quarrel over that piece of land. People saw him pull his pistol, but it wasn't over the land, was it Quatie?" She nodded. "He was trying to protect Emmet. Take care of her," he said to Des. "Quatie, I'll tell Josh."

"Tell me what?" Shank said from the door.

"The killer is Emmet Bell," LeFevre answered.

Josh stepped to the side of the bed. His long fingers reached into the shirt pocket and pulled forth the strip of silk. "You wear silk petticoats, Quatie?" he asked.

LeFevre made a face. "Well, I'll be damned, Joshua Shank. I never thought you was interested in ladies' undergarments."

"I'm not, but I found this piece of silk where Quatie was attacked."

LeFevre and Shank looked at Quatie for the answer.

"No. I'm sure I wasn't wearing a silk petticoat."

"She was wearin' one," Des said from behind the men. "I washed it this morning, but it didn't have no hole like that in it. Look for yourselves," she said, pointing to the little room where Quatie's bath was.

Shank snatched the garment down and brought it to the others. They examined it, turning it, hunting for a tear. There was none. The silk fragment was also a mellower white.

"Emmet Bell was the only boy I ever knew who wore a silk shirt," Shank said.

Chapter Eight

Des shooed LeFevre and Shank from the room and began to fuss over Quatie, changing the sweat-soaked gown. The two friends, at LeFevre's pace, walked down the stairs and onto the veranda. The sound of frogs and crickets, the smell of honeysuckle and roses drifted over the summer night.

"Did you find the Adeyaheh?" LeFevre asked, stretching his leg out and lifting it to the bench beside him.

Shank nodded affirmation. Leaning against a wrought iron column he looked into the night.

"He had a shack up Sleepy Creek toward Warner-ville. I found him laying on the floor with his head blown away. Spent most of the afternoon getting him over to Frank Starr's place and taking a letter to Orpheus' sister."

"Orpheus kill him?"

"Why? He was hiding him up there, bringing him food, taking messages to his folks."

"Hell, Josh, I'm just askin'. But if McKee didn't kill him, who did and why?"

Shank turned and sat on the banister facing Le-Fevre. "Will, if Quatie's right then Emmet Bell is here somewhere in town only we don't know him. He's moving easy with the Silam lot. He's not putting any restraint on himself. He's lost all control, killing the three girls, the Adeyaheh, and maybe Orpheus because he's gone, too. But I'm sure he'll want Quatie before he's through. I'm sure he came back to Shiloh for her and just couldn't pass up the children that night. He'll want her to suffer or else he'd have killed her last night when he had the chance. You've all got to stay togeth-er here while I try to find him."

"The U.S. Marshall won't do us any good if it's Emmet," LeFevre said. "Listen, Josh, he must be watching what's going on, listening to the talk. He knows who's tracking him by now. Susan and Noah aren't safe either."

Shank froze. His wife and son were alone, miles away in the night.

"Stay with Quatie, Will. Don't leave her alone," Shank said over his shoulder. "I'll bring my family over here in the morning for you to keep while I find that bloody bastard."

"Ma, I don't want to go to sleep. I want to talk to Pa about the stranger," Noah protested Susan's tight tuck as he wiggled in his bed.

"Shiloh's full of strangers, Noah. Thee can talk to thy father in the morning. Now thee must sleep."

"But Ma, he wasn't just a stranger. He was in our barn. I seen him."

"Saw him," Susan corrected as Noah shoved a bare foot out of the tucked covers.

Before she caught him, he had skipped across the room to the window. "See, he was right over there, just comin' out the door."

"Noah, thee is being willful. Get in this bed." She caught the eight-year-old firmly and drew him to the bed. "Thee will sleep. I will tell thy father, and if he thinks it important, he will wake thee." The boy seemed contented with that. Susan blew out the light and went to the door. "Good night, Noah. I love thee."

Susan walked down the well-scrubbed stairs. She stopped at the landing, looking at the parlor door that stood wide open.

"Josh?" she said. "Josh, is thee home?"

No answer came, and Susan moved quietly down the stairs. The parlor was empty, and she looked at the porch as she closed the door. A crash like something hitting the kitchen floor made her jump.

"Josh? Is that thee?" She moved into the empty dining room and placed her hand on the swinging kitchen door. Gently she pushed it open. The brindle cat was sitting in the middle of the kitchen table. A vase of wildflowers lay crushed on the floor.

"Bad cat. Bad cat." Susan chased the tabby out the open back door, then stopped as she realized the door had been open. Once again she checked the porch as she closed the windowed door. "Oh, Josh, where is thee," she said to herself as she backed into the room.

"Right here, Susan," Shank's deep voice said.

Susan jumped, caught herself and leaned back against the door with a racing heart. Her gentle eyes flashed.

"Why is thee sneaking about on cat feet in the middle of the night, leaving doors open so the animals come in?"

"I didn't leave any doors open, Susan. But the wind is up. Maybe they blew open."

Susan was on her knees picking up the broken vase and flowers. "Thy supper's stone cold," she said. "The wind is getting very clever these days turning door knobs on opposite sides of the house."

Josh caught her up and held her close, turning her face up to his. "Does thee have cause to be afraid? Has something made thee afraid?"

Running her fingers along the button panel of his shirt front, Susan looked down and sighed. "No. It's the town and you being away so late and Noah's imagination."

"Noah. What's Noah done?"

"He says he saw a stranger in the barn."

"When?"

"This afternoon while I was at the store. Look," Susan drew Josh to the window. "Noah saw him in the spot near the hay behind the wagon."

Shank bent and studied the moonlit barn. "Susan, did thee leave a lantern burning out there?"

But before she answered Shank was out the door and running. He jerked up the bar holding the door and pulled, but the heavy door only creaked and would not open. Shank ran to the creamery. The door was wedged shut. He bolted around the side of the barn toward the other broad doors. He threw the bar and pulled with his strength, the muscles were tight and hard in his body. The doors gave, opening into the inner hall. Fire.

The calf was loose and running about, panicked by the flames. Josh sprang toward the stalls, untied the mules and fanned their rumps toward the open door. He caught the cow by her halter rope and dragged her from the stall. The calf was gone and the mother cow balked, planted her feet and lay back, eyes rolling, against the rope. Shank pulled harder, using all his strength against the beast.

"Susan," he called to his wife, who stood now at the door. "Hold her while I get the calf."

In his arms, Shank caught the kicking calf, falling to the floor in the struggle. He showed her to the old cow, and he and Susan led them into the night and penned them away from the burning barn. Shank returned for the wild-eyed horses. He threw a blanket over the head of the last one who froze in terror before the blaze. He tied her to the porch and joined Susan at the pump.

Pushing her aside, he pumped until sweat poured from his body. He filled the buckets she brought, grabbed two and rushed toward the barn. He threw the meager water against the scorching fury, then turned to go back. Susan threw her bucket. Shank saw her skirts were afire. He caught her, knocked her to the ground and began pounding the flames with his bare hands. He rolled her against the ground, picked her up and carried her to the porch. Dropping onto the steps, Shank and Susan watched the new barn collapsing beneath the flames.

The bell of the volunteer fire wagon clanged the firefighters from Shiloh into the yard.

"Let's go, boys," Tom Bryan shouted. "Hank, form a bucket line from the pump to the barn. Bill, bring the hose wagon over here. We'll spray the porch and save the house."

Moving behind the pumper, Susan and Shank watched the townsmen scurrying about the yard tossing water against the lost barn, straining on the pumper handle of the fire wagon. Each minute more men arrived, yelling, taking buckets and blankets to the fire patches that lay around the barn and yard.

In a little while, the human energy was drained and the burned barn smoldered and hissed into ashes. The men rested about the yard, drinking long drinks from the water buckets boys carried. Coffee cooked on a safe fire in the yard as Clary Bryan and Susan poured it into cups. Clary even had managed to find a few donuts. Some men began to leave as they saw the cause lost.

Bryan tossed a kerosene can at Shank's feet. "Looks like we've got a barn burner in Shiloh," he said. "I'm sorry we weren't more help, Josh. The smell of smoke woke me too late. I'm getting too old for this. Half the men in the neighborhood got here as soon as we did. Kids were even out chasing us."

"Susan," Josh yelled across the yard. "Susan, has thee seen Noah?"

"No. Oh, no." She dropped the coffeepot she held.

Shank took the stairs two at a time and threw open Noah's door. The curtains fluttered in the open window. The boy's bed was empty.

Chapter Nine

"Susan," Josh said, "Susan, get thy bonnet and shawl."

He turned her from the empty room and gently pushed her down the hall toward their room. He paused at the top of the stairs watching her disappear and listening to the voices from the porch.

"This ought to show him, and you, you can't trust an Injun no matter how fine he's educated. Don't matter how long a dog's pedigree, he'll still roll on a stinkin' carcass. Same way with an Injun. They ain't to be trusted." The voice belonged to Jud Lewis.

Bryan said, "You folks are always free with an opinion you aren't asked for, but I didn't see any of you helpin' fight the fire."

"My boys and me was out interrogatin' some Injuns. Couldn't get here sooner."

Josh stepped onto the porch beside Tom Bryan. He did not ask the Silam posse to dismount. Across the yard he watched Clary Bryan pour the last hot coffee onto the ground.

"Everything as well as can be with you, Shank?" Lewis asked. Shank nodded. "Understand you was a busy boy this afternoon taking that dead medicine man to Starr, carrying a letter to McKee's sister. You know what that makes you to me and all the folks who knows what that killer done. You got just what you deserved this night, Injun lover."

Shank stepped up to Lewis' horse and caught the bridle. He fixed Lewis in his clear blue gaze and spoke in a steady quiet voice that only the sheriff could hear. "Lewis, men like you don't understand reasonable talk, but maybe you can get this. You and your boys haul ass out of here, and don't ever come back. Don't ever go near Minnie McKee again or you'll deal with me. Do you understand?"

He released the bridle, and Lewis whirled the horse and rode into the night.

Bryan watched Shank take the bridle and saddle from the grey and turn her loose. He threw them on the sorrel tied to the porch and began to rig a bridle out of the tie rope for the bay. Josh worked quickly and when Susan came out the door, he lifted her onto the sorrel.

"Josh," Tom said. "Susan can ride in the buggy with Clary and me."

"There isn't time, Tom. I've got to take her to LeFevre. She'll be safe at Pin Oak." Shank walked back into the house. Bryan followed him.

"Safe? But Josh, we can keep her with us or take her there tomorrow. This barn burner won't come back tonight."

"Tom, there isn't time. Someone has taken my boy." Shank lifted the Winchester from its rack and left the house. He swung up onto the bay's slick bare back. "I've no time to explain, Tom," he said. "Let's go, Susan."

Bryan put his arm around Clary's ample waist as they watched Shank and Susan gallop into the darkness.

The night ride was hard, but Susan clung to the saddle and did not slow the pace. Shank explained the situation as best he could while they rode. Finally he slid off the bay and helped her onto the horse block at Pin Oak. George stepped from the shadows of the porch with a Winchester in his hand.

"I'll need a fresh horse, George," Shank said as he opened the door for Susan. "Upstairs," he said to her. They hurried through the elegant entry toward the stairs. Susan had never seen Pin Oak before, but she did not pause to consider the house.

Upstairs, Will LeFevre sat by Quatie's bed with a shotgun across his lap and a Colt revolver in his belt. He lowered the gun when he recognized Shank and Susan.

"Where's Noah?"

"He's gone. Bell burned the barn and carried him off in the confusion."

"Goddamn," LeFevre said under his breath.

"I'm leaving Susan with you, Will. By the time I get back home, there'll be enough light for tracking."

"Wait, Josh," Quatie said from the bed. "Des will make you a grub sack in a few minutes. You mustn't get weak." Des left the room even as Quatie spoke.

"Quatie, this is Susan," Shank said, drawing Susan to him.

"I've heard many fine things about you," said Quatie, sensing the Quaker woman's anxiety for her son. "We are glad to have you here with us. Noah will be found all right."

Susan nodded and smiled, but clung to Shank's hand. LeFevre saw the Winchester in the Quaker's other hand.

"We'll take good care of Susan," he said. "Josh— for all our sakes, don't hesitate to use that gun." He saw Susan tremble and clutch Josh's hand tighter. "Be careful, old friend."

"Horse's saddled," Des called up to Josh. He turned, kissed Susan's cheek and went downstairs. Des handed him the bulging food bag. "Keep you strength up, honey. And don't worry 'bout these folks here. Me and George and Little George ain't no fools." She lifted her apron and drew an old cap and ball pistol partially from her skirt pocket. "God didn't make no fools around here."

Emmet Bell was not a woodsman. His trail was clumsy, easy to see. Shank could tell that Noah was giving him a hard time. But Bell had gained time during the fire and Shank's ride to Pin Oak. Bell also knew what he had in mind, where he planned to go, what he planned to do. He was more than a match for Shank. And once he reached Devil's Legion, the advantage was his.

Shank pushed the horse into the brush below the caves. Yesterday, a hundred years before, he had followed the Adeyaheh here and lost him. This time he rode the horse past the trail up the mount. He circled around the sloping end and across the broad ridges toward the river that ran from the caves. The country was rough, and the horse began to foam with the work. Shank did not let up. Time was his enemy. A moment lost in care for the animal was a moment lost to his son.

The Quaker was a good and gentle man. Hardness was not his way. Yet life forced him into decisions, paths that had to be taken. He had no philosophy now. He was working his way, step by step. His values were not forsaken, but were to be tested and weighed and refined in the crucible of the long summer day.

At last, he reached the stream. Shank dismounted and unsaddled the spent animal. Pulling the bridle from the gelding's big head, he stroked the soft pink muzzle. Taking the Winchester and putting the cartridges into the oil cloth grub sack, he waded into the water and toward the rock wall where the stream merged with the underground river.

The river was deceptive. It appeared to run along the side of the mountain back to Shiloh and Sleepy Creek, but below here it was stronger and wider, fed secretly by the underground water that poured from beneath the rock. Shank and LeFevre had found the entrance as boys exploring their hills. Everyone knew of the cave and the river, but none had followed it out. The boys had fancied themselves explorers and had kept their knowledge to themselves saving it for a special time. Shank used the secret now, grateful to the past, those easy days of playing explorer. He ducked into the water just at the rock wall, held his breath and pushed off the bottom rocks against the current. He swam under the rock ledge fifty feet, then raised his head in a small antechamber, caught his breath and plunged into the water again. At last he reached the cavern and hauled himself onto the rock floor. He pushed the straight wet hair from his eyes and fumbled to open the grub sack.

The contents of the oil cloth bag were dry. Shank drew forth the cartridges and a napkin. He had put in a box of shells and matches at his house in the early dawn. Drying the chamber and removing the tubular magazine rod, he began to wipe his Winchester with the cloth napkin. He dried the gun the best he could, then loaded it and levered a shell into the chamber. He pushed the boxed cartridges into his belt and stood up. He then made a torch from a piece of driftwood, and, holding it high, he studied the room. Everything was as it had been the day before, silent and empty.

Joshua Shank began the climb to the cave's mouth on the mountain pathway. Room by room he retraced yesterday's journey. Room by room he found the river cave empty.

At Pin Oak morning found LeFevre drinking scalding coffee from Quatie's fine bone china. The shotgun rested in the bend of his arm. He studied the back lawn falling away into Sleepy Creek and checked the woods beyond. The house was vulnerable from all directions. The broad balcony and high glass doors would give easy access to any room. Inside Quatie slept in her high bed, and Susan tossed fretfully on the cot Des had set up at the foot of the bed. LeFevre had to keep the women together. He could not move fast enough to protect one out of his sight.

He heard Quatie yawn and went inside. Susan was awake too, sitting up primly in the dress she had come in. Des backed through the door with a tray laden with breakfast and coffee. She sat it down on the table and pulled chairs out for Susan and LeFevre.

"Here, Miss Susan, you eat you something," Des said. Quatie reached for her robe. "Not so fast, you ain't. You stay in that bed, and I'll bring you something to eat." Quatie settled back as Des handed her a damp rag. "Wipe your face and hands. My but it's a nice cool morning. Fall's coming early this year." She set a bed tray across Quatie and brought food and coffee from the table. "Eat all that," Des told her.

Quatie stirred the coffee idly, looking across the room at LeFevre and Susan. No one said anything, but all their thoughts were on Shank, somewhere far beyond the safety of this room.

Finally LeFevre spoke, "We'll all stay in here together. Little George is on the roof and George is outside keeping watch. If it looks like trouble, you women will go into the dressing room. I can guard that door easiest. Nobody leaves the room but Des. Understand?" He looked at Susan and Quatie. They nodded. "I expect Bell's gone to the caves. That's where I'd go. Josh knows them like the back of his hand. Really all we have to do is wait. Josh knows what he's doing. He knows every inch of those caves, doesn't he, Quatie?"

Quatie knew LeFevre was talking to comfort Susan. Susan was an outsider here. Shank had gone back to Pennsylvania to court and marry her. She did not know Shank's childhood, that LeFevre and Quatie had shared. Talk of that past time might take her mind from the Quaker schoolteacher who was now stalking his deadly quarry on the mountain of caves.

"We used to play all over that mountain," Quatie said. "We kept bloody knees crawling through those dark passages. It's a wonder we never got lost. But if it was a new place Josh made us take a string or mark the walls. He always had the best sense of us. But I don't think he liked the caves. He just watched out for LeFevre and me. Isn't it funny the dangers kids get into and out of without a scratch? Angels must stay very busy watching over children."

"I remember one time they nearly didn't," LeFevre said. Quatie frowned slightly, but he didn't notice. "It was the summer after your brothers were killed and your daddy ran us boys off and sent you away. That summer it was just Josh and me. We played we were explorers and set out to find where the river came out of the cave. We climbed all over the mountain and couldn't find a thing.

"Finally, Josh said we'd just have to swim out with the current. We didn't know how far the water ran under the rock or if the opening was big enough to let us out, but we cut some hollow reeds and peeled off our clothes. The water was cold as ice, but we waded in and got caught in the current. My god, it was cold and fierce. I sucked in water through my reed and nearly drowned. I still remember fighting for breath. Josh pulled me up in a little low room, and we got enough air to swim out. Josh never lost his head. Not ever that I remember. It was pretty bad times here after you went away, Quatie."

Quatie's eyes were filled with tears. She blinked, tossed her head slightly and lifted her chin. LeFevre knew the gesture. He had seen it years before when she had cut her leg on a barbed wire fence in front of the boys; when her father had caught them smoking down by the creek; and when he had run him and Josh off for good and without a chance to pick up their things —the things hidden away in Quatie's chifferobe. From the bushes, he had watched Carter Rose jerk Quatie up by the arm and drag her looking back up the hill to the house. He had seen her cry. She must have slipped back for their toys.

When LeFevre had finally sneaked up to the house the next day, Des had told him Quatie was gone, gone away to school. Mr. Carter didn't want his daughter hanging out with a bunch of backwoods boys. LeFevre loved her even then. He had gone to the creek every day and sat looking at where they had played. He had thought of her soft touch and the beauty of her among the wildflowers and sunshine. He had remembered her fearlessness before the snakes that made him go cold inside. Without Josh he'd have never gotten through that summer.

He didn't see Quatie again for five years. It was Christmas and Carter Rose let her come home. The old man holed up in the library and got roaring drunk. LeFevre had a present for Quatie, a gold locket. He had taken it to the kitchen, and Des brought Quatie down, grown and beautiful. He gave her the locket and self-consciously kissed her cheek. The old man yelled somewhere in the house and LeFevre jumped away. But Quatie caught his arms and kissed him softly on the lips. That was her present, and he carried it with him for years. He'd seen that strange defiant little gesture then too, as she turned and went to her father. There had been a lot of trouble at Pin Oak that year. He heard the combat between Quatie and Carter Rose even down by the creek.

The next time he saw the gesture, Quatie stood in the witness box refusing to say more than that she had killed William Bell and shot his wife and son. LeFevre was a lawyer then, hammering on the facts that witnesses saw Bell draw his pistol first and knew he was trying to swindle her out of Carter Rose's Arkansas land, that Bell would do anything to beat the Cherokee mixed blood.

"Quatie," LeFevre now said, "You never told at the trial why you killed William Bell. Don't you think it's time to get things straightened out?"

Chapter Ten

Susan looked startled, taken back by the straightness of the question between these friends. She felt she had no place here. These were Josh's friends, companions of his youth. She was only here because he had brought her here to wait for him, for her stolen son. She was an intruder. She had not earned the right to hear these words. Yet she wanted to hear, wanted to know why Shank and LeFevre stood by this murderess.

"I didn't mean to kill Senator Bell. I went to Silam for Emmet. And they all came out of the theatre together. I pulled the buggy in and stood up to get out. I saw Emmet step behind his father and I said something like, 'You goddamn coward. You child raping coward.' I reached back in the seat for the snuff box I had found by my sister but as I turned I heard a bullet smash into the leather seat. The horse reared and threw me on the ground. I had the Winchester in the buggy. I got hold of it by the barrel as I fell. Puffs of dirt kicked up around me as Bell kept shooting. I felt my side burning where his bullet hit me, but I couldn't get to my feet. I kept struggling on the ground.

"Finally, I had the gun right; I cocked it and fired. He grabbed the center of his vest. I could see blood beneath his fingers, under the gold watch chain. He threw his other hand into the air, and his gun flew up and behind him. India Bell picked it up as he was falling and fired over his body toward me. She must have hit Emmet in the leg, it wasn't me. She shot again, and this time so did I. It hit her in the hip. Suddenly men were grabbing my gun away and holding me. It felt like it had lasted forever, but then it was over. I could hear people yelling for the doctor. Sheriff Duncan carried me to the jail."

"What's this talk?" Des asked. "You, William Le-

Fevre, did you start this talk?" Des had come back for
the trays and stood in the doorway with hands on her
hips and fire in her dark eyes.

"No, Des," Quatie said. "It's time to talk about it. If
I'd not been too ashamed, too sure that only I would
kill Emmet, maybe those three children would be alive.
Josh wouldn't be out looking for his son now."

"What did thee hide? Why did thee want to kill
anyone?" Susan asked quietly. Quatie dropped her
head, studying the backs of her hands.

"She had reason, good reason," said Des. "And
that's enough said."

"Susan," Quatie said looking up. "When I came
home after Papa died, I had an eleven-year-old sister.
Her name was Millie. Her mama was George's sister,
Cordelia. When I was sent off to school, Papa moved
Cordelia into my mother's room, her place. That first
Christmas I came home, Will, when you brought the
locket, I found out. I was furious, displaced by my
father's lust and loneliness. What was worse, Papa
wanted me to take the child for a servant, as if she was
not his blood or mine. He cared nothing for her or her
mother, yet he sacrificed my love and respect to have
them. I could not understand. It seemed unfair, an
affront to decency to hold life so cheap. It betrayed all
I had been taught. The precious virtue he demanded of
me, he did not believe in. He was a phony.

"We fought all Christmas. I packed and left for
Europe planning never to see him again. I never for-
gave him. Probably still don't. I hated him in every
man I met. I trusted no one after that. I was gone for
six years and came back after his funeral.

"Millie was still here. Her mother was dead, and
Des and George were raising her. She was a beautiful
and loving child, but I hated her as the fruit of my
father's betrayal and for her Negro blood. I was proud
of the Cherokee and my white blood, but I hated to
think of Negroes mixing with our blood. I know that is
hard for you to understand. You Quakers have always
looked at the person and not the color. But we were
raised to fear Negro blood, to be ashamed of it, to
avoid people who were what they called tainted with

that blood. I don't know why I never questioned that, why I accepted it. Maybe it began too early in my life for me to be conscious of it as a thought separate from me. At any rate, I didn't want her around. I didn't want to see her or hear her voice. I wanted to send her off. But there was no one to send her to. Besides I had been sent off, and I'd sworn never to do that to anyone, to solve any problem. I just dreaded to do that to anyone. I hoped I would find courage to do what was right and love her as my sister. I knew what was right, but would not do it. I was threatened, afraid of something I couldn't name. She wanted and deserved my love, but I withheld it."

Quatie got up and walked toward the desk, seeing and describing a day seven years before. Tears ran down her cheeks unheeded.

"One day Millie was playing here over by the chifferobe while I wrote letters. She had a puppy and was giggling and bouncing about. I seethed until I finally sent them both out. I was angry beyond any reason and paced about until I decided to go for a ride. George brought a horse, and I rode for hours. I don't know where I went. But when I came home, it was getting dark and ground fog was rising along the creek. George wasn't in the barn to take my horse, although he had the buggy horse hitched for my trip to the theatre that evening. I had to put my horse away myself.

"By the time I got to the house I was wild again, and Des too was gone. Little George said Millie was lost down by the creek somewhere, and they had gone to look. The child had ruined my plans again. I burst out the door and down the slope determined to thrash her for this outrage.

"In the distance I heard George and Des calling her. I went the other direction into a boggy bottom where I'd seen blackberries that afternoon. I walked for a long time, blistering out Millie's name.

"At last I heard her voice calling me, crying. It circled through the mist to me. I couldn't tell where it came from. For some reason it scared me, and I wasn't angry anymore.

"When I found her she was laying under the blackberry bushes. Her dress was torn and covered with mud. Her mouth was bleeding and bruises covered her face. She was way back under the bushes. She put out her muddy hand for help. I didn't want to touch her.

"She called to me again, and again. I lay down in the mud and took her hand. Pulling her out, I picked her up and started back calling for Des and George.

"When we got her into the house, we saw what had happened. She was so hurt, so torn. She kept crying, trying to tell us something. I pried her hand open to wipe it clean and a silver snuff box fell on the carpet. Inside it said, *To Emmet, Love India.*

"Des worked on Millie, quieting her, washing her. George went into the gunroom and got the new Winchester. He shook all over. But Des wouldn't let him go.

" 'Who you gonna kill, black man?' she cried. 'Where you gonna get justice for this child? You ain't! You ain't gonna do nothing but shame her more and get yourself killed.'

"I took the gun and went out to the buggy. I don't remember the drive, but I must have gone very fast. By the time I got into town, I saw the crowd leaving the theatre."

Quatie came back to them then, turned from the desk and looked at LeFevre.

"You know what happened then. All the anger, all the hatred of my life came out that night. I tried to kill all the unfairness in myself and the world.

"But Quatie, why didn't you say anything about Emmet at the trial?" asked LeFevre. "You'd never have gone to prison. We wouldn't have lost seven years."

"Will, do you think Emmet Bell would have been punished for a crime against a Negro girl? Bell's lawyer would have made it look as if she attacked him, as if he were the victim. And the jury's prejudice would have done the rest. Millie would have been worse off. In the morning light, the thing was to get well, to heal ourselves. Maybe I thought someday I would get another chance at Emmet to kill him without hurting

Millie anymore. Maybe I thought that. Maybe I was just burned out, too tired to talk."

"Where's Millie now?" Susan asked.

"Over there." Quatie nodded through the window toward a grassy green hillside where her mother, brothers and father were buried together. "She never recovered, just became more and more frail, Des said. She died the second winter I was in Detroit."

"Oh, my," Susan whispered. "Josh is out somewhere thinking to kill Emmet Bell, and my own heart doesn't think that so wrong. But it is wrong. It is wrong to kill, to even want to kill. I wish I had my book."

Quatie reached into her bedside table and brought forth a Bible. It was a cheap prison Bible, soiled and much used. "They gave me this when I got to Detroit. It's not very pretty, but the words are the same. Perhaps you would like to use it."

Susan took the book and moved toward the little dressing room, to be as alone as their common threat would let her be.

"Just a minute, Susan," LeFevre said. "What you said about wanting to kill. I don't think it's wrong. I don't think Josh is wrong. I think it's right to want to destroy something bad. It may be wrong to take its destruction on ourselves like Quatie did, but even that book you're holding provides for the cleansing of society from wanton meanness. It prescribes exceptions and rules for witnesses and for evidence. But it doesn't say a wanton murderer is to live or even to claim too much of our pity no matter how bad his own life has been. If we give in to that pity, we deny the human being's right to choose his life, to be human at all. Hard as that may seem to us, we have to affirm right sometimes by destroying wrong. It may be a negative way, Susan, but we can't save a killer without denying his victim. Some things are worse than death, things like being a slave, or living in a cesspool where nothing has any value, where life is cheap. Sometimes real love has to be tough, too.

"Maybe if Quatie had killed him; maybe if she hadn't feared the weakness of the law to act; maybe if the law wasn't weak and impotent because of the weaknesses of men; maybe if we all didn't hesitate to make the hard choice, maybe Bell would have died as he deserved and three little girls would be playing in the sunshine instead of lying in their graves. That's a lot of maybes. But it could be we aren't to be sure. It could be that we have to keep trying to find answers instead of resting on untested theories, humane or hard. Life's trying to find the best answer to the problem with the facts we have, Susan, not the perfect answer."

"Will," said Quatie. "You ought to be a lawyer."

"I am a lawyer."

"I know," Quatie said softly. "I know."

LeFevre suddenly felt uncomfortable. Here he was defending uncertainty, the right of the law and people to sometimes make mistakes in trying to do what was right. Anybody could make the nice and pleasant decisions in a perfect world. That wasn't hard. That was easy. But people don't live in a perfect world, and they only grow when they choose between what may be equally undesirable alternatives and live with the results. Had Quatie known that as she stood there in the witness box? How had he missed that and drunk away seven years wanting the world to be always true and perfect, the dream of a boy child playing by the river bank?

"My god, LeFevre," he said to himself and sat down.

Chapter Eleven

Joshua Shank blinked against the strong daylight as he emerged from the river cave. The pathway before him was steep and rough. More caves black and perhaps empty were ahead. But somewhere up there on the mountain were his son and a killer. He leaned into the climb.

The morning was quiet and still. He could almost hear the very air as he passed through it. A Quaker morning, Susan called it. Josh didn't think about being a Quaker now. He only listened and climbed. He had thought before about killing McKee, about killing all the killers and being done with it. But he had rejected those thoughts. He had refused to betray the still small voice—until his barn burned and his son was taken. He had obeyed through other people's sorrow but now, when it was his turn, he picked up the gun as easy as other men. He did not think highly of that. He did not think highly of Joshua Shank. He knew there was something up that mountain waiting for him that was worse than anything he had known or imagined. He did not think. He just climbed, wanting to face himself and Emmet Bell and see what they would do.

All through the afternoon Shank searched the caves. They were black and cold away from the summer sun, empty labyrinths running into the corrupt mountain like termite tunnels in dead trees. In one hole he found a cup and bedding. Bats squeaked out of others.

Josh walked the trail carrying the gun loosely in his left hand. He was alert to every sound, every light and shadow, every movement. Anything out of place caught his attention. Once he saw a flip of white movement under a ledge, the tiny movement of the breeze against something. He kneeled. Under the ledge a rock weighted a torn bit of paper with writing on it:

Come and find me, Shank. If you can.

Shank left it, barely stopping to read it. He wanted
Bell. He wanted him before his reason came back;
while he still hated him.

Another hour passed. Deep in the middle cave
Shank lifted his torch. The light fell on emptiness, but
sitting on a rock ledge another piece of white paper
drew him.

Come and get me, Shank. Kill me if you dare.

Shank crumbled the paper and threw it to the stone
floor. He stalked through the cave and into the light.
Now Emmet Bell was playing the cat, and Shank did
not like being the mouse.

Shank kept climbing, crawling into the small caves.
He came to the top in late afternoon. None of the
spiraling caves had held his son or Bell. Shank stood
looking about. From the top he could see three coun-
ties besides the towns of Warnerville, Shiloh and Silam.
Below him everything seemed small, far away. Above
him was only sky. A beautiful place, but Shank had
never liked the clearing. The clearing was a sad place,
a place corrupted by some suffering he could not
place.

"Tired, Shank?"

It was a chilling voice. Emmet Bell stepped from
below the jutting cap rock and walked up the grassy
slope toward Shank. He carried a shotgun in the ready
position. "Brought *thy* gun I see." He did not hide his
sarcasm.

"Where's my boy?" Shank gripped the Winchester
tighter, then set it on the ground, butt first against a
rock.

"Ashamed to think like other men, Quaker?"

"Where's my boy?"

"Here. There. Hard to tell, Josh."

In two quick steps Shank crossed the space to Emmet, shoved the shotgun aside and slammed his iron-
hard fist into Bell's patrician jaw. He fell like a stone

and lay shaking his head at Shank's feet. Then he smiled.

"Nice right for a Quaker."

Shank reached down and pulled Bell to his feet. He drew back his fist again ready to smash the smirk from Bell's face.

"I wouldn't hurt him, Josh. I love children. But you might hurt him. You might kill him, if . . ." He waited for Shank to ask the "if."

"Get on with it."

"If you don't bring me Quatie Rose, I won't tell you where he is, and he'll die buried in this mountain where you'll never find him. You already passed him once, Josh. You didn't find him, did you?"

Shank looked at Bell. He was a little man, barely taller than a woman but tougher, hard and sinewy. His hair was short like Quatie said after her beating. And he wore a soft silk shirt beneath his summer broadcloth jacket. He looked foppish even here on the mountain. He did not look like Emmet Bell the fat mama's boy Shank remembered. The self-indulgence had grown in the past years into a lean sinister selfishness. Nothing mattered to this man but his own way. There was an emotional coldness in his eyes that precluded pity or reason.

"Where's my boy?" Shank shoved Bell away and kicked the shotgun out of reach.

"Bring me Quatie, and I'll tell you," said Bell, sitting carefully on a fallen log and looking at his long neatly manicured nails.

"Why do you want Quatie?"

"We have business to finish. Look what she did to me." Bell opened his shirt revealing long scratches where her nails had dug into his neck and chest. "She's a vixen, that one. We could have settled things the other night, but Orpheus McKee interrupted our meeting. Poor Orpheus so quick to defend a lady. So dead. By the time I finished with him, you'd found Quatie and carried her away. You spoiled my plan.

"See what butting in has gotten you, Friend Shank? If you'd have let things be, I would have just finished my business with Quatie and left her. Gone my own way. And your little son wouldn't be buried alive. You see what Quatie caused, the trouble she's caused you. You ought to hate her, not me, Josh. You ought to bring her to me without thinking twice."

"Your thought process always amazed me, Emmet. My son's life can't be purchased at the price of another life. That's not even an option. He's not for sale. Besides, you can't expect to walk away from here leaving three children brutally murdered, three families broken. It's not just my son to trade, it's a girl killed seven years ago and three more this week and how many others? And it's justice."

"Oh, but it is just your son. Think, Josh. Your son's seven or eight maybe. His life's ahead of him. Quatie's a convicted murderess. She got off light for killing my father. She hasn't paid for causing my mother to grieve herself to death. She deserves justice."

"You don't give a damn about justice. You just want her for your private hate and because she's the one person who can tie you to the campground killings. Your past isn't safe with her around. You knew she'd figure out who the killer was. And this time she'd tell. But killing her or even me won't make you safe. People know you're not dead; you can't kill us all. You should have stayed away, Emmet. You should have let it lay."

"I couldn't stay away when I heard she got out. I knew she was free, walking around free. I'd wake up thinking about it at night. She wouldn't have believed I drowned. She would have come for me. I had to put chairs all around my bed at night so she couldn't sneak up on me. It was simple self-defense to come here."

"Was killing the children self-defense?"

Bell shrugged. "Things got out of hand. I didn't set out to kill them, but I remembered that nigger girl Millie. She told Quatie. Nobody'll ever tell on me again."

"I don't understand you, Bell. I don't see how a man could do what you did to children. Why, Bell? Do you even know why you kill little girls?"

"Little girls turn into big girls. I get them before

they grow up, while they're still fresh. Before they can hurt me."

"Hurt you?"

"Here's the facts of it, Josh. Women are out to destroy men. If they see any chance, they'll take it. They push a man to the limit, like India, sweet mother, did my father; and then they turn around and slap your hands for using the wrong fork. I hate women, I hate them," he almost whispered. "They never let up."

"You killed Orpheus and the Adeyaheh, too. They weren't women."

"That's right. Had to kill McKee. He just kept coming. I wanted to bring him in for a fair trial for killing the children, but he wouldn't let me. It was lucky I happened along in time to save Quatie, or he'd have killed her for sure. Of course, by the time I got back, she was gone. I hunted for hours but finally gave up when I was jumped by that old Indian medicine man. He kept chanting and shaking rattles and potions at me, calling me a witch. Splattered his stupid face all over the cabin. 'Course I had to do it, him being McKee's accomplice and trying to kill me. I wouldn't have done it otherwise."

"Who are you talking to, Emmet? A minute ago you admitted you beat Quatie. I know you. I know you killed Orpheus and Adeyaheh and it wasn't self-defense."

"That depends on how you look at it. McKee was in the cave that night. He could have remembered something, put things together with the old man's help. Besides he got in my way with Quatie."

"And the old man. What did he know about the killings?"

"He always knew I killed them. He knew about Quatie's nigger sister. He saw me leave her in the blackberry thicket. He kept quiet because I was a witch, but mostly to get Quatie sent to Detroit and out of his hair. She and the other damn white Indians were ruining his game. But he saw me in Warnerville a week ago. I could tell he knew me and was figuring out a way to conjure me and make the old gods look good.

Then after the accident at the campmeeting I knew I had to find a way to get rid of him. It all fell into place very easily. Even Quatie, until you came along. Now I have to punish you."

As he talked, Bell moved toward the guns Josh had shoved aside. Josh watched his movement.

"We're going back, Emmet. The law has to deal with you. I can't, I despise you too much."

"Oh, really, Shank," Bell said. "You bore me. If you take me to town, I'll never tell where the boy is. Nobody will ever find a body. He'll just perish of hunger and thirst and then turn to dust."

"When you're in jail, I'll cover this mountain till I find him. Let's go."

"Get Quatie or shoot me. I have nothing to gain by going to Shiloh and nothing to lose by dying here." He inched closer to the shotgun. "How lonely it must be to die buried alive with people all around and nobody can find you. How lonely for your boy."

He grabbed for the gun, but Shank was ready. He caught Bell with a right to the stomach, sending him back against a boulder. But Bell didn't stay there. He lunged at Shank, using his head as a weapon against the tall man's midsection. Shank staggered and slipped to one knee. Bell moved in, driving his fists into Shank's head. Shank fell forward, and Bell drove his knee into his face. Struggling to stay conscious, to hold his attacker and recover, Shank circled Emmet's short thick legs with his arms and let his weight fall against him. They fell hard and rolled over each other, landing blows that spent energy, but had little effect. Then Shank forced himself up and pounded a right and a left into the face of Emmet Bell, who finally fell back, unconscious. Shank sat on his middle, ready to deliver another blow. Slowly, he stood up, watching Bell for any twitch. Shank stepped away and began to brush at his clothes. Bell was out, really out.

Shank saw the broad brimmed hat that he'd lost in the fight. He walked over, stooped and picked it up. Brushing back his hair, he put it on. Then suddenly Shank whirled at the noise behind him—the dry mechanical click of a shotgun being cocked.

"Look at me, Shank. Look very close. See my face. I want you to remember me and know you killed your own boy. You killed him to save Quatie Rose."

Bell opened his mouth and took the gun's barrel between his teeth. Shank yelled and started toward him as Bell pulled the trigger, blowing his own head into a pulpy mass that exploded into the air, against the rock and Shank.

"My god," Shank sank to his knees. "Oh, my god, Emmet."

Chapter Twelve

The light in Quatie's room cast a warm glow over the twilight. Quatie played checkers with LeFevre, who held his shotgun across his lap. Susan read under the lamp's painted globe. They heard the doors downstairs burst open. All three looked up at the noise, LeFevre grabbed up his gun.

"In the closet. Now!" he cried, and cocked the gun as the women moved. Then he laid the barrel on the table, holding it at the height to blow away a man's guts.

"Don't shoot, Will. Don't shoot! It's me—Josh." Shank opened the door carefully. And LeFevre uncocked the gun. Quatie and Susan came out of the dressing room. They all stood looking at Shank. His shirt was ripped and dirty, splattered with Bell's blood and brains. His face was bruised and there was a cut over one eye. Susan gasped and grasped her waist.

"Where's Noah?"

"I don't know. We've got to find him. Bell's dead, and he wouldn't tell me where Noah is. Susan, I want you and Will to go to town for help. Quatie, come with me."

"Let me come with you," Susan's blue eyes pleaded with him. He drew her close to him and stroked her soft auburn hair. "Quatie knows the mountain like I do, Sue," he said.

Quatie had already slipped into the dressing room and was putting on rough clothes as Des came to the door.

"Tell George to bring the dogs and horses," Quatie said. "I can dress myself."

Shank spoke solemnly to Susan and Will about what had happened on the mountain. His voice had no energy, his face no emotion. Finally he said, "You must tell Tom Bryan and Frank Starr, tell them we need them, every man, woman and child who'll come. Noah's hid somewhere in some hole. Oh god," he put his face in his hands.

"I'm ready," Quatie said. "Josh, is there anything we can use for a scent for the dogs?"

Shank looked up. The words were clear, but somehow did not quite penetrate his mind. "Scent? At home. We'll need something of his. Susan, you'll have to go home and bring us a shirt or pants, anything. Will, can you get help alone?"

LeFevre nodded. "I'll get them there."

"Des can help Susan and bring her to the hunt camp," said Quatie. "Let's go."

George and Little George had saddle horses ready for the men and Quatie. George handled the dogs for Quatie. Little George quickly readied the buggy for Des and Susan and hopped aboard. The black woman grabbed up the reins and slapped them onto the horse's sleek back. "Run, you hoss. Make tracks."

The friends separated on the missions the night held for them—Shank, Quatie and George to the mountain; Susan, Des and Little George for the shirt; LeFevre for help.

"Josh, take it easy. We can't start the dogs till Susan comes. You need to rest," said Quatie, stroking her mare's silky side and loosening the girt. George had already tied his mount in the trees beneath the mountain. He gathered wood for the hunters' fire that would burn through the night as the men listened for the treeing bay. But tonight there was no sport; there was no joy at the fire, the night or the throaty bays.

"Quatie, I've got to find him. He's got to know I'm here. I've got to be close to him, as close as I can get."

Quatie watched George light the fire and roll up a log for a seat. "Josh, you can't help him if you don't get some rest. It won't be long until Susan comes. Till then you should lie down by the fire and sleep. George and I'll be awake and watching." She handed him the blanket roll from her saddle. He took it and went toward the fire.

In a little while, Josh Shank fell asleep. Exhaustion from the past three endless sleepless days caught him at last. He had not slept since the night Quatie came into his parlor with talk of following the Adeyaheh. For two days he had tracked men and saw them blown into lifelessness. His hands ached from the unaccustomed blows of today's fight. His new barn had burned, and his animals roamed about untended. His son had been carried off and was being buried alive somewhere. But for the moment, Shank was too tired to act. Tired, but not alone.

Will LeFevre slid the horse to a stop before the stone stairs of the church. In moments, he was inside laying his full weight against the bell rope until the night rang with the sound of bells. The posse men from Bryan's store were the first to come. LeFevre could see them jumping off the porch, silhouettes against the warm light inside the store. He saw Tom come out too, untying his apron. But he kept at the rope, wanting the sound to call in the townspeople and the farmers and Indians on Shiloh's edge.

"What the hell's goin' on in there?" Jud Lewis' voice spat into the summer night. "Come out here. Goddamn I can't think with them bells ringin'." He said to Latta, "Get him out here."

Latta caught LeFevre from behind and jerked him away from the rope. LeFevre fell shoulder first against the wall. Unsteady on his broken ankle, he struggled to get his footing.

"Outside, drunk," Latta said and reached for him again.

LeFevre turned and drove his fist into Latta's soft belly. The Silam thug doubled up with the force as LeFevre shot a quick short blow into his chin then stepped back to watch him fall. LeFevre glanced out the window at the growing crowd. He reached for Herb Latta's shirt collar, dragged him to the porch and rolled him off at Lewis' feet. "Next time," he said, "come yourself, Sheriff."

"What's wrong, Will?" asked Tom. "Why are you ringing the bells?"

"Folks," LeFevre said. "Josh Shank's boy is lost over on Devil's Legion, buried alive somewhere in the caves. We need everybody who can walk or crawl to help hunt him out."

"Let's go," Pettigrew Willis said, and the Shiloh men began to move.

"Anybody needs lanterns or rope, come by the store and I'll give 'em out to you," Tom Bryan said.

"Just a minute." It was Jud Lewis. "Just a damn minute here. Before I go off on a drunk's words, I want to know what's going on."

"There isn't time to choose sides, Lewis. The boy's been gone since last night," LeFevre answered. "If you can't see the need of helping, don't come. As a matter of fact, you weren't invited, Lewis. For all the help you've been so far this whole town could go to hell. All you have done is strut around with a mob of white trash terrorizing the Indians and making a bunch of fools believe they were too big for the little town we built here together. All you've done for us is turn us into a bunch of pack dogs taking on a downed pup. And you've made the law an ass. Now you're telling us to wait and explain things to you while the best man in this town is about to lose his son for want of help. To hell with you."

LeFevre stepped off the porch and into his stirrup. "I'm going to get Walker and Starr. The rest of you go on to the cave pockets. There'll be a fire at the hunter's camp." Suddenly LeFevre reined in his nervous horse. Across the heads of the milling crowd he saw Frank Starr and Ross Walker riding before the Cherokee into the yard of Shiloh Meeting. A blanket-wrapped body hung from the mule the men led. Walker and Starr eased through the crowd to the church porch as the other Cherokee circled the edge.

"We have brought you Orpheus McKee," Starr said. "We want to know who among you claims the honor of shooting a man in the back and cutting his throat? Who takes the credit?"

The words echoed over the citizens of Shiloh, and men began to look at each other, to ask the questions of their neighbors.

"Don't matter how he died or who killed him, Injun," Jud Lewis shouted. "He's a murderer. He got what was coming."

"Orpheus didn't kill the children," said LeFevre. "Emmet Bell raped and killed them just as he did Quatie Rose's sister seven years ago. He came back to shut up Quatie when she got out of prison, but he found the children first. He's the killer. And he killed himself this afternoon in front of Shank after burying Noah on Devil's Legion. Now, for all our sakes, let's get out there and find that boy."

Little George galloped up to the fire. Quatie stood up. "Where's Mrs. Shank?" she asked, taking the shirt he held out.

"They're comin' in the buggy. But I was faster so I catched up a horse and rode ahead."

Quatie smiled. "You did good, George. Go on back. They'll need you." She gently shook Shank awake. "We're ready, Josh. Little George brought the shirt."

Shank jumped, got himself awake and stood up. "Let's go."

George held the shirt under the wet black noses of Quatie's mixed brace of shepherds and hounds. The pack breathed deep, taking the scent as Shank led them to the mountain path. The dogs spread out, nosing the rocky soil and bushes. The leader Jezebel hunted slowly for the boy's smell. She snuffed and coughed in irritation as she could not place the scent. She snapped at a pup who got too near and broke her concentration, then put her nose back to the trail. The humans watched her, hoping, believing in senses they did not possess or understand.

"Come on, dog," George said as he waded among the lesser hounds and held the firebrand to see better.

Jezebel yelped and ran up the pebbly path. Her deep bay flowed from her throat and filled the still air. The other dogs took it up. The night electrified with the sound. Quatie jumped with anticipation. Shank ran after the dogs.

Jezebel ran hard, strong on the scent. She ducked into a cave and began to search for the way. As Shank came to the doorway, she came out.

"Here, girl, in here," he said. But the dog only looked at him and turned away up the mountain.

"Come on, Josh," Quatie said. "She knows what she's doing."

The woman and the men followed the dog, watched her search the path and lead them higher. She held on the scent ignoring the pack and people, drugged by the olfactory pleasure of the hunt. Finally she went into the middle cave, circled the entrance and took a passageway.

"Hold the dogs here," Shanks said to George. He called them up and snapped leashes on them. "Come on, Quatie."

Quatie and Shank walked back into the passage after Jezebel. Their lights flickered and bounced on the cold lifeless walls. The dog's tail wagged gaily as she led the way. The room was not more than eight feet across. Shank had been here in the afternoon. He saw the note laying on the floor. Jezebel sniffed furiously then bounded onto a rock. Shank and Quatie watched her slip and fall behind it. She did not reappear. The pair looked at each other and moved toward the spot. They stooped, wanting to see, then heard the full thick bay.

"She's got him, Josh. She's got him."

"Can you see in there, Quatie?"

"I'll try." Quatie squirmed between the big rock and the wall. "Here, Jez'," she said. "Come here, girl." The dog's head finally appeared in the small hole. Quatie struggled to pull the leggy dog out and lift her onto the rock. Shank lifted her down as Quatie bent and tried to see into the opening. She pushed and shoved herself into position, trapping her arm beneath her. "Hand me the lantern, Josh." He lowered it, and Quatie held it into the darkness. "It's long and narrow, a little tunnel as far as I can see. I'll have to crawl inside to see any more."

"Come out here first."

Quatie handed up the lantern, then squirmed and wiggled her way back to her feet. She stood up and rested her elbows on the rock before the final push over the top.

"I've got to move this rock," Shank said. "We can't get back in there this way. How'd Emmet get Noah in there?"

"Maybe he drugged the boy so he could handle him or maybe he made him crawl in and then followed him. But then how'd he keep him there?"

"Tied him up. Help me, Quatie," Shank leaned into the rock.

Quatie shoved hard, putting her back against the wall and pushing with her legs. Sweat stood on Shank's forehead as he threw his strength against the rock. It did not give. "Call George," Quatie grunted.

George came quickly, set his torch in the rocks and joined Shank and Quatie. The three heaved against the stone, and it began to move. A last push, and it rolled away from the two-foot hole.

"Give me the light," Shank said. "I'll go in and see."

Quatie gave him the lantern. He put it ahead of him and crawled on his belly inside the hole. His boots kicked toward Quatie and George's faces, but then almost out of sight they stopped. Quatie heard his voice, but not his words.

"Get his leg, Miss Quatie," George said. "He's stuck." Quatie and George pulled Shank from the hole.

"It's too small. I can't get to him." His voice was soft and hollow.

Quatie looked at George. He was an inch or two shorter than Shank, but he was heavier. He was too big, too. "I'm not too big," she said.

Shank considered Quatie. She was small enough to get through. She had grit. She could carry Noah. If muscle was needed, he and George could supply that by rigging a rope around Quatie.

"Get ready, then," he said. "George, we will need the rope from the horses."

"Yes, sir! Here it comes." George slipped off after the lifeline.

Quatie stripped off the jacket she wore and tossed it aside. "What could you see?"

"It's just a tunnel. But I think there must be a well or pit or turn back there because the light glanced off a wall at the back. Crawl in on your stomach. The light's back as far as I could reach. Just get in, take it easy, see what you can see. We'll decide what to do when we know. Quatie, I called Noah's name. I think I heard something move."

George didn't take long with the rope. In minutes the line was secured around Quatie's waist, and she crawled into the tunnel. She used her elbows and legs to move. She could not stand or crawl on her knees. Inch by inch she went toward the light and the mystery beyond. The lantern's smoke filled her eyes and nostrils. She ducked her head to her hand to wipe her eyes. Then she crawled on, pushing the lantern ahead. She began to call Noah's name and listened to her voice sliding along the stone walls.

"Noah!" she called out again.

"Here, here I am."

Quatie clawed her way faster toward the distant sound. She held the light forward an arm's length and tried to set it down, but found no ground.

"Here. I'm down here," Noah's voice was sharp and clear.

Quatie crawled another two feet, feeling the edge of the void with her fingers first, then looking over into the well. Noah stood twenty feet below, looking up toward the light. His fair hair and movement drew Quatie's eyes.

"Hello, boy," she said. "Are you all right?"

"Yes, ma'am. I'm not hurt, just scared. My candle burned out. And my stomach hurts from that junk he made me drink."

"Well, don't be scared. Your daddy's outside, and we'll get you out of here before a cat can wink his eye. I'm going back now and tell him you're here. So hold on just a little longer. I'll leave the light, Noah."

Quatie reached across the well to a rock outcropping and set the lantern securely against the wall. "Noah, are there any snakes in there?"

"I don't think so. No, there ain't."

"I'll be right back, boy."

Quatie kicked back down the crawlway. She backed out and sat up, turning into the room. Susan and Des were there.

"He's fine, just fine. But he's got a stomachache from something Bell made him drink." Susan hugged Shank upon hearing Quatie's news. "He's in a well, twenty feet down. I'll have to go down for him. You'll have to haul us up. I don't think I'm strong enough to climb out with him."

Quatie crawled back into the tunnel faster and surer. When she reached the well she studied the best way to put her legs over the side. Finally, she drew them up tightly under her and inched to the lip of the hole. She caught a rock projecting from the rim with her right hand then her left and pulled. It held. She eased herself out of the tunnel and put her weight on the rock until she was stretched out. She felt the rope lowering her slowly toward the boy. She walked the walls as the rope men carefully eased her down.

"Hello, Noah," she said, looking over her shoulder. "Are you all packed?" He grinned and Quatie stood down on the bottom. The lantern above didn't give much light, but she saw the grin. "If you don't mind, I'd rather not stay to dinner." She picked him up, adjusting him in relation to the rope. "Put your arms around my neck, your legs about my waist and hold on, boy. I don't have many active muscles." She tied him to her with a length of rope she carried, then tugged on the line running back to Shank. "Let's let your daddy work from here on."

Slowly they rose out of the stone well toward the light, toward the tunnel. At the top Quatie pushed Noah up into the crawlway.

"Get going, boy. Your mama's worried," she said lifting herself out of the well.

Noah scrambled quickly ahead. By the time Quatie reached the opening he was already in Susan's and

Shank's arms. LeFevre had arrived and he extended his hand to help her. She took it and stood up as he drew her into his arms and kissed her.

"I forgot the lantern."

"Forget it. We need to practice this." He kissed her again, and she returned the kiss. "Wait," he said. "I didn't hear you say you'd marry me."

"I didn't hear you ask."

"That's settled then," LeFevre said. "You know Susan's a minister."

Quatie laughed and drew LeFevre limping to the door of the cave and into the night. "I need air. I hate being shut up in holes. Look at that," she said as Susan and Shank, carrying Noah, emerged beside them.

Below and around them the mountain was alive with lights—tiny dots made by torches and lanterns danced before them. The people of Shiloh, white and Indian, had come to help.

"Isn't it beautiful," said Susan.

"Yes, we're all together again," Shank said.

Tom Bryan and Frank Starr stepped out of the path, offering Shank their firm handshakes. Bryan held Shank's arm. The sound of boots crunching on rocks made Shank look up the mountain away from the lights. Whiting and men from the Sisco Mortuary were bringing down Emmet Bell's blanket-wrapped body.

"People can go awfully wrong when they've got clenched fists," Quatie said as they passed.

Tom Bryan nodded. "One good thing though. Folks found out we need each other, even if we are different. You showed us that, Josh, when you wouldn't take sides or let Jud Lewis poison your mind. You just kept on helping people. They had to come help you. And when they did, they knew that was the best way. Son, you're a genuine fistkiller."

Cynthia Haseloff was born in Vernon, Texas and was named after Cynthia Ann Parker, perhaps the best-known of 19th-Century white female Indian captives. The history and legends of the West were part of her upbringing in Arkansas where her family settled shortly after she was born. She wrote her first novel, *Ride South!*, with the encouragement of her mother. Published in 1980, the back cover of the novel proclaimed Haseloff as 'one of today's most striking new Western writers.' It is an unusual book with a mother as the protagonist searching for her children out of love and a sense of responsibility, rather than from a desire for revenge or fame. Haseloff went on to write four more novels in the early 1980s. Two focused on unusual female protagonists. *Marauder*, of the two, is Haseloff's most historical novel and it is also quite possibly her finest book. As one review put it, '*Marauder* had humour and hope and history.' It was written to inspire pride in Arkansans, including the students she had known when she taught high school while trying to get her first book published. Haseloff's characters embody the fundamental values—honor, duty, courage, and family—that prevailed on the American frontier and were instilled in the young Haseloff by her own 'heroes', her mother and her grandmother. Haseloff's stories, in a sense, dramatize how these values endure when challenged by the adversities and cruelties of frontier existence. Her talent, as that of Dorothy M. Johnson, rests in her ability to tell a story with an economy of words and in the seemingly effortless way she uses language. Haseloff once said, 'I love the West, perhaps not all of its reality, for much of it was cruel and hard, but certainly its dream and hope, and the damned courage of people trying to live within its demands.' Her latest novels include *The Chains of Sarai Stone* and *Man Without Medicine*, both published as Five Star Westerns.